99
days
with
you

99 days with you

CATHERINE MILLER

Bookouture

Published by Bookouture in 2019

An imprint of StoryFire Ltd.

Carmelite House
50 Victoria Embankment
London EC4Y 0DZ

www.bookouture.com

ISBN: 978-1-78681-889-8
eBook ISBN: 978-1-78681-888-1

Written in memory of my good friend, Tim Galea.
May he be forever 27.

Nathan's Diary

I, Nathan Foxdale, have always been twenty-seven. For as long as I can remember, whenever someone has asked my age, my instinct has been to reply twenty-seven. The reason? The dream I find myself trapped in. It's pinning me to that age. But only now, on the eve of my birthday, is it nearly true.

Twenty-seven seems a nothing age. No significant rite of passage. No roundness to the numbers. And yet this is the year I've been waiting for all my life. The one in which I die.

It is a strange thing to be able to say with the utmost certainty that you know your expiry date. Especially when the reason for that belief is a silly recurring dream. But I've dreamed it so frequently that I can't believe it's not true. I am on the eve of my final year and I can do nothing about it other than live like every day might be my last.

Chapter One

Emma

Emma Green didn't normally start her mornings like this. The usual ritual was pretty set in stone: her alarm set to assist her mother's daily drug regime, limiting the time she had for getting ready herself. But today she was lingering, stark naked, in front of the full-length hallway mirror, her long, dark brown hair covering her shoulders while the rest of her remained bare.

It was okay. Emma knew her mother's mobility prevented her from stumbling upon her nude daughter. In fact, stumbling stopped her mother from doing a lot of things. Living, mostly.

Emma turned to view herself in profile. This way, with her left side to the mirror, there was nothing to see. She looked normal, though admittedly with a little bit too much body fat for someone still in her twenties; the only kind of workout she got these days was lifting her mother's legs into her bed at the end of the day.

The clock in her head, used to the many demands on her time as she got ready for her job each morning, reminded her not to dilly-dally. She turned once more – away from her reflection, to avoid another frontal view. She didn't need a second look from that angle to know something was amiss.

With her right side now in profile, Emma braved a peek. Sweeping a finger along her skin, she traced the curve of her breast. It reminded her of the head of the antique doll her mother kept in her bedroom, its strange unblinking eyes always keeping watch on her.

Emma reversed the sweep. The roundness uninterrupted. The difference to her other side so abundantly apparent. Blinking, she stared at the mole nestled near her areola. The flat nipple. The one that hadn't perked up for three days.

Just this once, Emma was ignoring her policy of being prepared for all weather conditions. After the naked showdown in front of the mirror, she tied her hair up in a loose bun and got dressed, opting for a flimsy blouse. It didn't stand a hope of being suitable for the rain. Even so, she tackled the stroll to the bus stop, oblivious to the chilling winds that would normally freeze her to the bone.

Today, she was stone. She wanted to feel what it was to be cold. Truly cold. Not wrapped in the many layers she would ordinarily wear when the wind was so icy, threatening sleet or snow at any moment.

On the short walk up Timberley Drive, she embraced the sensation. How those layers had stopped her living, if it was only now she was experiencing the bitter cold for the first time. The hairs on her arms stood on end – and oh my, how abundant those hairs were now she could see them fully – and her teeth chattered, but how she wished she'd done this before.

Only it wasn't working. And the chillier she got, the clearer it was that even the ice-cold wind and the rain weren't enough to make her nipple bud into life.

By the time she finally turned the corner onto the main road and reached the bus shelter, she'd never felt more alive. Maybe now she would appreciate those crazy people who wore shorts even when it was pouring with rain.

Glancing down, she peered at the sodden blouse clinging to her bra: the left breast with its pronounced response to the cold, the right steadfast in its decision not to react.

'You alright, love?' An elderly lady, shopping trolley in tow, was braving the rain in a weather-beaten coat. It must be nearly nine o'clock if the bus-pass brigade were out. That meant she was late to work. She was never late to work.

Normally she would engage in polite conversation, but today she couldn't bring herself to respond.

'It's just you look like you're on the walk of shame.' The old lady giggled. 'I do hope he was worth it, love. You shouldn't be dressed like that in this weather. You'd best get yourself home soon, dear, before you catch a cold.'

With that, hot tears cascaded like a waterfall Emma was powerless to stop. Her breath caught and she gasped in a lungful of freezing air so sharp she let out the yelp of a wounded animal.

'Oh my, sweet. I'm so sorry. I didn't mean to upset you. No man is worth any tears,' the lady said, offering comfort in all the wrong places.

Emma gathered herself together. 'Thank you,' she replied, not really sure what she was thanking her for but looking for something polite to say before she fled.

It was no good. Emma wasn't going to be able to face work today. She needed to do the thing she'd been putting off. She would get in touch with her GP. She would stop burying her head in the sand.

Running away with her face to the sky, she didn't care if she tripped or if anyone saw her. She wanted the rain to drum on her skin. She wanted to feel the elements.

She wished this was a walk of shame. That this morning she'd left the toasty comfort of a double duvet, having spent the night under the crush of a man's body. That she'd left a note offering her phone number, but not really expecting any kind of follow-up. That she'd been brazen enough to take to the streets with smudgy make-up and stale perfume, with barely a thought to her one-night stand.

Instead (and she was pretty certain about this) she would be the woman who would lose her right breast before she would lose her virginity.

Chapter Two

Nathan

It was a rule for Nathan Foxdale that life should be lived hard and fast and without fear. Though the secret truth was that Nathan loved the fear. That rush of adrenaline he got every time he jumped out of a plane wasn't the buzz of being alive; it was the ever-present dread of The End. The not wanting to waste a day. That was the fear: that if he wasn't living life to the full, he was in danger of not living at all. That fear was what had propelled him to spend years travelling the world. It was what had eventually led him to settling back in the UK, for the skydiving he loved.

It had been a while since he'd done a solo jump. His job usually involved having someone strapped to his chest, embarking on the adrenaline high of their life. It didn't matter the person, their terror was always palpable, some needing far more reassurance than others.

This morning, AirFly had four instructors and only three clients, so he had a rare chance to parachute without having to guide someone through those anxious moments of flight and the awkward manoeuvre towards the open door, 15,000 feet above the ground.

It was Derek giving the pre-jump talk today. It was always an overload of the senses for those taking part. While they were trying to listen to critical information about how to land their jump safely, they had other instructors circling them, ensuring all the safety checks were complete; that goggles and leather hats were on correctly and straps were done up right.

Nathan was always able to sense the tension in the air, and even though he had done this hundreds of times, every single time he was aware of the overwhelming presence of that feeling. It was part of the lure of this job. Not only did he get to enjoy the adrenaline highs of what he did, he also got to absorb the static energy created by the anticipation.

He knew the talk off by heart, having given it himself more times than he cared to think about. Today he concentrated on enjoying the experience, taking his time over getting ready for once.

He hauled his jumpsuit on and carried out the safety checks on his own parachute. The other instructors were both close friends of his: Tim and Antonio. They'd all been on the jumping circuit a while and it was a tight-knit community. Sitting at the reception desk behind them, Leanne, Tim's girlfriend, was keeping the business ticking over. It was a fairly tight ship, but then it had to be, given the kind of work they were in.

Finally, happy the parachute was as it should be, Nathan shifted it onto his back and secured the fastenings.

'Ouch!' He said it out loud without meaning to, causing the entire group of instructors and clients to shift their attention to him. It even gave Leanne cause to move from her usual spot at the reception desk.

'Are you okay?' she asked, her face full of concern.

'I'm fine. Just caught myself.' Nathan rubbed his chest.

'Do you need me to get the first aid kit?'

'Honestly, I'm fine.' He wasn't really sure if he was, but he didn't want any fuss.

Derek, the owner of the company and the oldest instructor, came over to check everything was okay. Leanne returned to her desk.

'You alright, mate? Not like you to flinch at pain.'

Nathan rubbed his chest. The ache hadn't subsided. 'Nipple hair,' he lied.

Derek grinned widely. 'There I was thinking you lads were all waxed and buffed these days. Put some ice on it if it's hurting. You can sit this one out.'

'Nah, I'm good. I just wasn't expecting it.'

'If you're sure?' Derek gave him a stern shift in the eyebrows expression before heading back to his client, who had the appearance of a lad about to pee himself at any moment.

Nathan wasn't sure, but he nodded all the same.

Now with a bit of space, he loosened off the straps and rubbed his pec some more. But the more he rubbed, the more he became aware of the source. A lump. It was small. Barely noticeable. But when his straps had been tight against his chest it'd been beyond any pain he'd felt before.

'You ready, Nathan? Time to move,' Derek called over in his direction, the last part of the tutorial completed.

'Sure,' he said, tightening his straps, careful not to set off the same pain he'd caused himself last time.

Despite having jumped more times than there were days in the year, he'd never lost count. Perhaps it was poetic that this was number 666. Maybe today's would be the last.

Each element of the skydive experience was always the same: the plane's ascent; the safety checks; the tension in the air; the order they went out of the plane; the things they said to their clients. It was all normal, the sky remarkably clear and blue for a January day.

Nathan was to go last, with no client strapped to his chest, shitting their pants. He liked to think that was a joke, but it had been known to happen. He was glad not to have anyone with him. The weight of that small lump pressing against his chest was quite enough.

It might just be a pimple. A spot that had reared its ugly head while he wasn't looking. But he knew it was more than that. Even without taking his clothes off to have a proper look, he knew something wasn't right. After all, wasn't this the thing he'd been waiting for all his life? It was always just a question of how the end would come. And here it was, in a neat, no-bigger-than-a-pea parcel.

When it came to the skydive, Nathan hesitated at the open door, like he always did. That sudden rush of air was enough to remind anyone what it was to be alive. That moment was the reason he did this job: he needed that affirmation.

As the aircraft juddered its way through the clouds – that impossible reality of a metal machine high in the sky – he did the count to three in his head and, as always, jumped on two. It was a bit of a cruel thing he did with all his clients – making them jump just before they were ready. It was his theory that if people always waited until they were ready, half of life's possibilities would slip out of reach.

For a few moments, he was dragged like tumbleweed through the air, the push of the wind against his limbs threatening to disorientate him.

It was the glorious sound of the air surging past him that Nathan loved. Everything about it shouted that parachuting towards the earth wasn't something anyone should do. That it was an act that should be beyond human capabilities. It was a sound unlike any other and it was only as he familiarised himself with it once again that the orientation of the earth became apparent.

In a beat of a second the clouds would part and the view below would become clear, the canvas of the landscape his to enjoy. There was nothing in the world that he knew to be so isolating and yet so exhilarating all at the same time. He was on his own, soaring through the sky, and for a moment, he closed his eyes and drank in the sensation. Before the descent got out of control, he spread his body out to steady himself against the wind that gushed hard against him.

Even in those moments of freefall, the pain radiated from his chest. The small insignificant lump he'd not known about an hour before created more noise than the wind he was sailing in.

This was when he should be counting.

The descent.

Knowing when it was time.

The right moment.

To open his eyes.

To yank the cord.

Let the rush of the unfolding parachute pull him skyward.

The move that saved him.

Every time.

Chapter Three

Every time.

As he moved closer to the earth, he wondered if he wanted to survive. Whether, if this were really to be his final year, it would be kinder to himself to let this be the end. Was it possible that this strange sixth sense he'd had all his life could be true? Or was he going nuts, considering ending his life over an insignificant pus-filled pore?

Below, the Salisbury landscape was a quilt of patchwork green, each field a slightly different colour to its neighbour, all stitched together by dark rows of bushes. The only buildings beneath him were dotted about randomly and looked like chalk marks on the scene. As Nathan grew closer to the view, he was no closer to wanting to pull the cord.

Living life at a hundred miles per hour meant it was rare to find quiet moments, and right now oblivion seemed inviting. Then he would never have to unpeel all the equipment, undress and give the tiny lump any further attention. He would never have to know, never have to fight a battle that he might not win. He would never…

See zebras in the wild.

Bathe in baked beans.

Run the London marathon.

Go on a murder mystery weekend.

Spend all night on a beach and sleep under the stars.

And all at once it was the right moment to pull the cord. Because if he didn't do it then, he would never get the chance to find out what tomorrow would bring.

It was time to live.

To fight.

To not be defined by the dream that kept him awake at night.

Chapter Four

Day One

Emma

The hospital letter had told Emma to bring someone with her. It was an obvious statement, given what she was facing. What it didn't state was who to bring in the eventuality you didn't have anyone to fill that role. She had always been the carer, not the cared for.

Of course, her mother would have come with her, if Emma had told her about the appointment, but it was an unnecessary worry at the moment and getting Carole to the hospital in her wheelchair would have added to the stress of an already anxious day. Besides, it might still be nothing.

Other than her mother, there was no one else on the happy-for-them-to-see-my-boobs-be-ultrasounded list. She'd considered her closest friend, Alice. But as she had her dad to care for and a younger sister to keep in check, she didn't want to add to her burden at this early stage. So it was a me, myself and I moment. One that she was taking for the team, even if it was making butterflies appear in quarters they'd never been before. Right now, every inch of her torso was aware of how hard her heart was beating, pushing itself to the limit in this unfamiliar environment. It would have been nice to have someone here with her, but some occasions were just better ventured into alone. She didn't think company would help her find the sense of calm she was hoping for.

Looking for distraction, she lifted a faded copy of *Woman's Fortnightly* from the paltry offerings on the waiting room table. She hated to think how many patients had leafed through the pages before her, but she was desperate. The clock on the wall was driving her mad with its insistent ticking. A constant reminder of how long she was going to be left wondering what was wrong.

The only other person waiting was a man similar in age to her. With his ruffled dark hair, he appeared to have come straight from work, wearing what looked like mechanic's overalls. He was handsome, with a rough-and-ready air, and seemed strangely out of place in the sterile waiting room. Presumably he was supporting his partner or mother or sister in their moment of need, during their breast clinic appointment. It was good that someone was here with an uncomplicated source of support. If only she'd managed to locate the same.

'Where's *Robot Wars Monthly* when you need it?'

He was speaking to her. Emma generally tried to avoid conversations with strangers. Partly it was down to her job at the library. There, she *had* to talk to strangers; it was part of her role. But the more years she'd worked there, the more she'd come to appreciate that a good percentage of strangers were weirdos. Or perhaps that was just where she worked.

'I'd say it's a bit specialist. Maybe lower your expectations and hope they have *The Sun*.'

The potential weirdo laughed. A features-creasing-up laugh, like she was actually funny. 'You think they'd cater for men a bit more, wouldn't you?'

'Ermmm…' She'd not really considered the quality of the reading material, or whether it met with equality standards.

'I guess they don't expect us here for appointments.'

Emma was rather flummoxed to be engaging in conversation with a good-looking man about the quality of the reading material at the breast clinic. It wasn't something she'd envisaged happening as part of today's visit. 'There must be lots of men coming to support their relatives. Maybe you should bring in your stash of *Robot Wars Monthly*. They're clearly in need of donations.' As she said it, she fanned the pathetic pages of the magazine, which was barely holding together.

'I think you're right. I'll add it to the top of my list of things to do.' He said it without sarcasm and the thought made her smile, even if she was pretty certain he'd made the magazine up.

He glanced around the waiting room, looking like he was at as much of a loss as she was. 'So, what magazine are you going to be donating? We need a bit of balance if the men are going to have plush new ones to read.'

She could have made up any title. Something exotic and exciting. Something racy. Something glamorous. But rather than embellishing her life, she told the truth and named the only subscription she had delivered. '*Carers United*.'

'Are you here with someone then?'

'I wish.'

'Oh. It's just – the carer thing… I thought, maybe… It's just, you seem young to be sitting here waiting for an appointment.'

'Apparently not. Although hopefully it's nothing.' Even though this wasn't a cancer clinic, they both knew what might be discovered behind these doors. 'So, who are you here with?' She didn't want to think about what was to come.

'You.'

God. Definitely a weirdo. 'I mean who have you come with?'

'Me.'

'I don't understand.' She'd heard of wedding crashers. Maybe even funeral crashers. But an appointment crasher was a new level of strange. There wasn't even a food buffet to try and freeload from.

'I'm the patient.'

'Oh.'

'Turns out men have boobs too.'

'And you're here by yourself?' Emma didn't know why she sounded so surprised when she was in the same predicament.

'Yeah. Turns out it's fairly embarrassing to admit to any of your mates that you need to be accompanied to a breast clinic. I figured I could handle an ultrasound by myself.'

'But what if it's bad news?'

'I'm pretty sure it's going to be bad news. What about you? Why is no one with you?'

The magazine she hadn't read fell onto the floor and it gave her a moment to avoid answering. She wasn't sure she would be able to if she was looking directly into his bright green eyes. He was a stranger. She didn't share details of her life with random men she met in waiting rooms. Even if they did have particularly lovely eyes. But then… Did it really matter if she shared? It was important that she didn't box her world in at times like these.

'The carer thing…' she began. 'My mum has been slowly dying all her life. She doesn't need to know her daughter might beat her to it.'

'Fuck. And there I was feeling sorry for myself. I guess you've already convinced yourself you're getting bad news as well.'

'I can't see it being anything else.'

A set of double doors swung open. Footsteps headed towards the waiting room. Papers were shuffled as medical notes were checked.

'Emma Green,' the uniformed woman called.

'I figure now is the time to find out.' She placed the magazine far too carefully on the table, as if the hesitation would make the inevitable go away.

'Anyone with you today?' the uniformed woman asked, with a polite glance towards her new weirdo stranger friend.

Emma glanced in the same direction and watched as he stood, as if it were his time to go in.

'I'm here.' Weirdo stranger wiped invisible dust from his overalls. 'If you need me to be, that is?' He looked directly at her this time.

'Through here.' The woman held the door open for them both. 'Partners are welcome to sit in for support.'

It went against every fibre in her body to even think about having a stranger in the room. She wasn't good at being intimate, even with those closest to her. She would always be the one slipping her bra on under her jumper in the changing room, never confident enough to be brazen. So allowing this new man in, especially when the ultrasound person was assuming Emma knew him, was the opposite of what her instincts would normally tell her.

But then this woman was a stranger, along with all the doctors and nurses and hospital officials she would meet over the coming months. So even though it was totally at odds with everything she was thinking, she returned the stranger's gaze and nodded. 'Okay.'

The woman led them into a room just off the corridor. In a better set of circumstances, Emma might have tricked herself into believing they were here for a pregnancy scan. Her partner with her to hold her hand as they saw their child for the very first time.

'You just need to take your top and bra off. There's a sheet there to cover yourself up with while you're waiting. I'll knock in a few minutes to check that you're ready.'

When the door closed, Emma froze.

'They've got a cheek calling that a sheet,' he said. 'It's the blue roll that the cleaners use, that's what that is.'

It made her smile, at a time when smiling should have been an impossibility. As if what she was facing wasn't enough to deal with, somehow she'd managed to rope herself into undressing with a stranger watching. 'What's your name?' she asked.

'Nathan. Nice to meet you, Emma Green.'

He extended a hand for her to shake, and she did. He had a solid, dependable hold, and all at once they weren't strangers. 'And as I'm such a gentleman, I'll be looking away throughout. I'm just here if you need a hand to hold or someone to talk to.'

'You know this means I'm doing the same for you,' Emma replied. She realised the moment she said it that must have been what Nathan wanted. It would seem they were both in need of some support after all.

'Well, naturally. I'm only doing this so I can cry on your shoulder like a baby if I need to later.' His smile wavered for a second. 'If I'm being honest, I'm really fucking scared.'

'Look away then,' she said. She pulled off her jumper and tackled her bra before slipping under the totally inadequate blue paper blanket. 'It's okay to be scared. I'm really scared too.'

There, she'd said it. She'd admitted to another human being that she'd been having kittens ever since she'd realised there was a problem. And somehow it was marginally easier to bear with her new weirdo stranger friend in the room.

Nathan's Diary

Everything in life has contrasts. The colours, the textures, the flavours. The way one person experiences something is entirely different to the next person. No two people have the same experience when they skydive. It is the same activity, the same drill that they go through, and yet so many things are different. Even for me. Sometimes it's the view I take in. How easy it is to notice the change of season when you experience it from 15,000 feet. Other times I focus entirely on the sensation of falling.

That's why I'm writing this dream diary… because there are things I don't understand about my dream. There's something about it that lacks layers. And yet I don't doubt it will come true. How can I, when it's the only dream I've ever had? What could be more convincing than something that reproduces itself in an exact duplicate most nights? A cast-iron statement of things to come.

In my recurring dream, I'm lying in a hospital bed, struggling for breath. I can hear a rattle and I'm aware of people in the room, but I have no idea who they are. I want one of them to be my mother, but as she is no longer on this earth, she'll only appear once the rattling has finally stopped.

So, I listen, wondering if each rasp is my last, one after another, and when they stop, that's when I wake. That's when I take a breath like no other. It's the moment I realise that, no matter how many times I have the dream, I'm no closer to knowing who's in the room with me. No closer to knowing if there is someone who loves me enough to hold my hand when the time finally comes. All I know for certain is that it's too soon. And there's nothing I can do about it other than keep breathing.

Chapter Five

Day Six

Emma

Emma had always seen working in the library as a passport to the world. Any career path she wanted to know about, any country she wanted to visit, any famous person she wanted to meet, they were all here in this one building, sitting on the shelves, hidden in the pages of countless books.

But as she carried out the mundane task of checking the Dewey Decimal Classification, ensuring each book was checked in properly on the computer system and returned to its rightful home, she sensed the passport shutting.

These shelves were no longer portals to other universes, they were a testament to the all the things she hadn't done.

In her hand was a *Lonely Planet* guide to Italy. She could take that book home and read it cover to cover, savouring the sights and sounds and smells of the country, but she might never go to Italy. For her, it might only ever exist in her imagination.

Just like she would never cook all the recipes out of *Mastering the Art of French Cooking* like she'd planned, as if she were starring in the movie *Julie & Julia*. She would never expand her voluntary work to another country, like Namibia. All the things she'd ever longed to do had warped into impossibilities overnight.

In a few short days, the walls of the library building had closed in enough to squash all sense of purpose out of her. She had a lifetime of nevers stacking up, and now she really would *never* get round to doing any of them.

She took the next book off her wheelie trolley and regretted it instantly. The full works of Shakespeare was a big enough volume to make her wince, and she wasn't able to keep hold of it. The thick tome landed on her toe with a thud, adding to the pain in her chest.

Emma closed her eyes, trying not to let everything get to her. There were so many things hurting and she didn't want it all to unravel under the duress of a whacked toe. Rather than shout out in pain, she swore under her breath and inhaled deeply before heading to the staffroom. She wasn't about to start crying out here, where she would be seen by staff and customers alike.

She didn't know anything yet, she told herself. There was still a chance it was benign. A very slim chance, but a chance all the same.

'Is everything okay, Emma?'

It was Trevor, her boss, blocking her route to the staffroom. And the question leaving his lips wasn't actually the one he was asking. The question he really wanted an answer to was: '*Why aren't you getting on with your job?*'

'I dropped a book on my toe.' Emma said it quietly, as if she were making an apology that she didn't want to be heard.

Trevor laughed. 'Hazard of the job, I guess. As long as you haven't broken any bones, you can at least pick it up. We don't want any customers falling over now, do we? Health and safety and all that.'

Emma glanced back at her abandoned trolley. She was unaware she'd left the book on the floor, its pages splayed in an ungainly fashion and its spine cracked in a position that would normally bring her out in hives. Today, she didn't care. Books could be replaced. Bosses didn't have to be arseholes.

'Go on then.' Trevor gave a definite nod and glare, as if she were a misbehaving dog that had not yet retrieved its stick.

'You pick up the frigging book.' Emma's voice was no longer quiet. It was loud and clear and made every punter in the library turn and stare.

Before Trevor was able to recover from his shock at her outburst, Emma turned on her heel, bypassed the staffroom and headed straight through the automatic doors to freedom.

Screw *never.*

Chapter Six

Emma

It took approximately two hundred metres for the wind to leave Emma's sails. What had gotten into her? Being rude to her boss and walking out of work were so uncharacteristic for her, she was sure they'd have a mental health nurse waiting for her when she got home.

Having marched out with an unprecedented amount of gusto, she quickly deflated to a standstill and had to find a bench to rest her woes on.

Her toe throbbed. Her boob throbbed. Her heart throbbed. Well, her heart throbbing was no doubt a good thing, but how long would that last if it turned out the lump they'd found was cancerous? The cancer specialist nurse had said it was more than likely malignant, so she wasn't holding onto much hope that the final diagnosis would be anything different. Faced with that, she would cope with her toe and boob ache as long as her heart throbbing continued. It was pretty essential after all.

And as it was still beating, she needed to work on screwing never. Which was a harder notion than it seemed when she needed to be back home for her mum by five o'clock. Heading off for a couple of weeks in Italy, sightseeing around Rome and eating some authentic Italian pizza and creamy, sugary gelato would help pass the time until the dreaded results arrived – if only it were a possibility, to just jet off and escape her worries. For most women her age it would be… But she had responsibilities she was unable to leave behind. So, other than walking out of work (which she might live to regret), she wasn't sure how to embrace life when she only had two hours before she needed to catch the inevitable bus home.

Glancing back in the direction of the library, Emma wondered whether what she'd done was sensible. Her practical side told her that she should just go back and apologise. But then she spotted Trevor outside the automatic doors, searching the crowds up and down the high street. He was looking for her. If she was going to die soon, she wasn't going to put up with any more of his shit.

Seeing Trevor propelled Emma into marching with renewed energy. *Screw. Never. Screw. Never.* Her feet beat the rhythm into the pavement. Screw staying put. Screw biopsies that didn't provide definitive results for two weeks. Screw life. No, backtrack, she didn't want to screw that. She rather liked life. Screw what life was throwing at her. That was more like it.

So invested was she in her own personal marching crusade that she didn't notice the A-frame on the pavement until it sent her falling arse over tit (not the best thing to do in her bruised post-biopsy state).

Glancing around to see if anyone had noticed, Emma got to her feet, using the frame for balance, dusted herself off and decided stomping around in a rage was clearly not the answer.

The A-frame had the answer: 'Champagne Afternoon Tea'.

Screw never having had an afternoon tea. Screw never having had the taste of sparkling champagne pass her lips. Screw never haven eaten fancy cream cakes and cucumber sandwiches.

Looking up from the sign, she spotted the hotel it was promoting and went straight in.

'Table for one?' the waiter asked when she entered the restaurant.

Emma nodded with far more confidence than she actually had. She was wearing black trousers and a pale pink blouse: her work garb. She wasn't dressed for a place like this, where she would be better off in a fancy tea dress. But it didn't matter. Finally she was being spontaneous – doing something she'd always wanted to do but had somehow never got round to. It was funny how life got in the way, right up until the point it didn't.

The waiter showed Emma to a table in a sun-filled conservatory that looked over the hotel grounds: an elegant pond enclosed in a courtyard she hadn't known about until now.

Each table had the cleanest, crispest, whitest linen she'd ever laid eyes on, and with the shiny cutlery and glistening glassware placed exactly as it should be, Emma was scared to move.

She did at least manage a smile when he came to take her order. With faux confidence she ordered a champagne afternoon tea for one. She said it like it was something she regularly did on an afternoon off, as opposed to a mad trolley dash round the supermarket before getting back to check on her mum.

When everything was delivered to her table it looked delicious. There were small finger sandwiches filled with salmon, egg mayonnaise and a mysterious substance she'd have to taste in order to identify. There were three pieces of cake: a glorious cream-and-jam-filled slice of Victoria sandwich, a mouth-watering piece of lemon drizzle and a chocolate tart that looked like it might have the ability to take her to heaven and back with a mouthful. Lastly, and rather triumphant in their size, were the scones. It was like they'd specifically scaled everything to make the scones look like the grandest there had ever been. All at once she felt more at home and tucked in eagerly, but after just a few mouthfuls of a salmon and cream cheese finger sandwich, her appetite disappeared.

It wasn't that it didn't taste nice. Or that the setting wasn't beautiful. But it didn't seem right to be enjoying this alone. She wanted her mother to be there. To be able to share it with her. If only the multiple sclerosis wasn't eating away at her, making things more impossible with each year that passed. The disease attacked the lining of the nerves, and each time it did, it stripped away more of Carole's abilities. She couldn't call her mother up and ask to meet her in town, the way she might have done as a teenager.

Failing having her mother with her, she just wanted to be able to talk to someone. She would have called her best friend, Alice, but she would be at work, and like her mum, she didn't want to worry anyone unnecessarily.

For all the ornateness of the room and the scenic view, it was rather lacking in customers. The only other people were an elderly couple too far away to make passing conversation with. Rather selfishly, she wanted to talk to someone about being scared without having to cope with the emotional impact it would have on them. She wasn't ready to think about that. Not yet. She hadn't even mentioned the appointment to Alice. She didn't want to burden anyone with terrifying concerns that might turn out to be nothing. Even if those thoughts were all she was able to focus on right now.

Instead, Emma took a sip of champagne and let the bubbles settle over her tongue. It was like a delectable honey with added fizz, pouring over her taste buds. The liquid sent a warm sensation down to her stomach and she immediately understood why people enjoyed this drink. She could certainly get used to it.

A few more sips began to restore her appetite, so she braved another sandwich, this time egg and cress that was so fresh the mayonnaise was still warm. When she dived into the heavenly looking tart it didn't disappoint for a second, its rich chocolate taste stripping away all her other senses while she savoured the indulgent flavour. Another sip of champagne and she felt braver still.

With no one to talk to, she got out her phone and opened up her messages. It was a very odd thing to think that she'd told no one else in the world about her lump other than Nathan. Ever since breast clinic day, they'd kept in touch. She already had a feeling they would see each other through many of the days ahead.

I swore at my boss and walked out of work, she typed into the small white box. She thought about adding *'Go me!'* onto the end, but she wasn't entirely certain her action had been one of her most rational moves.

Emma pressed send and then checked to see when Nathan was last online. She didn't know when he would answer. He might be high in the sky right now, about to jump out of a plane. She'd learned a lot about his job as a skydiving instructor as they'd waited for him to be seen. He'd told her about how he'd got involved with every adventure sport he could when he'd travelled the world, and it was the desire to earn money from what he loved that had landed him his job. He'd told her how he had an affinity for the sky over the sea, much preferring jumping into thin air than the ocean. His life was infinitely more exciting than her part-time job as a library assistant, where she'd only ever jumped head first into books.

After a few moments she knew he hadn't seen the message, so she returned to her afternoon tea and decided to tackle a scone, slathering it with jam and cream.

More than likely he was jumping out of a plane. As far as 'screw never' was concerned, he was the kind of person to put her rather mild afternoon tea into perspective. But at least it was a start.

Chapter Seven

Nathan

The rasping from Nathan's dream had come to haunt him in real life. No matter how hard he tried to catch his breath, he wasn't able to. And while there was never an ideal time to feel like he was dying, having a stranger attached to him made it perfectly awful timing.

The door to the plane was open, with the first of the recruits about to make their jump. It was normally the point when he'd be pumping out overly jubilant remarks about how this was going to be the experience of a lifetime to the nervous candidate awaiting their tandem jump. Instead, he was pretty certain he was in the midst of a heart attack.

The pain in his chest was increasing. A sensation like pins and needles was radiating up his neck and face to the point he started seeing stars, white spots filling his vision.

If the hospital had carried out a biopsy like they had for Emma, then he could understand it. She'd had to sign a form with a bundle of potential complications listed. Fatal blood clots had been one of them – which tallied with his symptoms. But he hadn't had a biopsy. They were planning to go straight for a lumpectomy to remove the lump that they suspected might be skin cancer, along with any surrounding tissue that might be affected, and that was still weeks away.

Nathan blinked, trying to rid himself of the blotches that were filling his vision. But as he did, his breathing became shallower. He felt like he was in his dream. Maybe it wasn't a hospital bed, as he'd always thought. Maybe the person he always saw holding his hand was in fact a total stranger strapped to his chest. At least it would mean he wasn't by himself when he died, even if it wasn't what he'd imagined and was miles up in the sky instead.

He suddenly realised that despite spending his whole life doing everything he could to live life to the fullest, the thing he feared the most was being alone. And it turned out he may have spent twenty-seven years being more alone than he'd ever realised. At the moment that thought passed through his head, the world turned black.

Chapter Eight

Emma

It turned out that middle-of-the-afternoon champagne wasn't conducive to full mental function. And that would have been fine – if Emma only had to worry about herself. The hazy headache started up when she was on the bus home, and by the time she returned she wanted to do nothing more than collapse into bed for the rest of the day.

Sadly, that wasn't an option. She may have filled her stomach beyond breaking point, but she still needed to sort food out for her mother. Fortunately, she'd made bolognese earlier in the week, so it was only a case of boiling up some pasta to go with it and dinner would be done.

As always, her mum was in the front room watching a quiz show. Everything she needed was in easy reach, so that she was able to live her life in this bubble of a house, confined to this room. Her bird-like frame jerked slightly as she adjusted position in her chair to greet her daughter. 'How was your day, love?'

'Usual,' Emma said. She should expand on the day, really. Let her mum know that she'd stormed out of work, had taken champagne afternoon tea on her own and, because she was so unused to drinking alcohol, was practically half-cut.

'No oddballs today then?'

Emma often relayed stories of the interesting folk that came into the library. Like Miss Red Coat, who came in twice a week to use the internet. She was about forty and was neatly put together apart from the fact she always wore odd shoes. Emma was yet to pluck up the courage to ask her if she knew that was the case. Then there was Mr Talkie-Talkie, who hadn't got his head round the fact that the library was a space for peace and quiet. She never used actual names, so it was never going to be a sackable offence. It was a window into the life her mother missed out on – a soap with a few regular characters. There were certainly some tales worth telling.

'Not today.' There might have been, but she'd been too busy sipping champagne and trying to pretend that everything was okay.

Everything was okay. Everything would be okay. These were the reassurances that were pounding through her thoughts. They weren't sticking though. The worry was edging towards her, minute by minute, rather than away.

'Not even Mr Anorak? He normally turns up on a Wednesday. I hope he's okay.'

'I think I must have missed him when I was doing the book club order. Lots of admin today.' The white lie fell so easily from her lips that it surprised her.

'Ah, that's a shame. His antics are always amusing.'

'I'll go finish dinner, if you're alright?'

'Thanks, love. Are you okay?'

'Tired.' Emma really was tired, and it took all the strength she had not to fall into a puddle on the floor.

Leaving her mum to the latest game show, Emma finished sorting dinner in the kitchen. Keeping herself occupied was a good distraction. As she laid the table, as always, she was reminded of setting up for a toddler. She set a mat down for underneath her mum's wheelchair, and a large spill-proof cloth across the table. It was easier to clean up this way, even if it wasn't particularly glamorous.

Over the past six months, Carole's myoclonic jerking had become markedly worse. The type of MS she had was known as primary progressive. And with every year it made itself more known. It was beginning to affect the routine of their lives far more than ever before.

Once she'd dished up the pasta, Emma wheeled her mother into place and regarded her with a sadness she'd not felt before. What if her results were bad? She had no idea how her mum would cope. She had no idea how *she* would cope. Everything suddenly seemed incomprehensible.

That sense of hopelessness lingered as she carried on with their daily ritual. In the same room where Carole watched TV, she prepared the bed for her mother, adjusting it so that she was able to get in with minimal help. Luckily it was electronic and she didn't have to manually get it to the right height and angle. She wasn't sure she'd be able to manage that right about now. She was drained of energy, simply going through the motions, the stitches pulling at her side.

After getting her mother and her Zimmer frame into place, Emma positioned herself nearby to help as required. They'd said after the biopsy for her not to do any heavy lifting for a week. It was fortunate that her mum was as light as a feather and mostly just required supervision and assistance with her equipment.

Once Carole had managed the shuffle over to the bed, Emma laced her hands behind her mum's ankles and swung them up. Carole was scrawny enough that the movement didn't pull on the stitches Emma had over her biopsy site. Her mind fast-forwarding to the worst possible outcome, she wasn't sure how else her mother would get to bed. She'd like to think her brother, James, would step in, but she was pretty certain he'd only offer to pay for help, rather than provide it himself. He'd already been at university when Carole was diagnosed, busy studying to become a financial broker. Over a decade later, his business had become so successful that he generally lived by the principle that there wasn't anything that couldn't be fixed with some money thrown in the right direction. If Carole or Emma needed help, he tended to pay for a solution rather than coming to sort it out himself.

How would her mother cope if treatment meant Emma wasn't able to care for her? Or worse, if she didn't survive the treatment at all? Those were the kind of logistics throwing her mind into overdrive. Because however hard it was, she'd always enjoyed the fact she was the one able to provide that care. She liked being the one able to give the support her mother required, rather than a stranger enlisted as hired help. It created a sense of dignity for her mum and strengthened their mother–daughter bond. She'd done it since she was a teenager, and however difficult it was at times, she knew that this arrangement made them both happy.

After she tucked her mum in bed, gave her a goodnight kiss and switched off the light, Emma retreated to her bedroom. It was a bookworm's haven. There was an entire wall dedicated to the shelving that housed her precious book collection. In one corner, she had what she'd classed as her reading snug, where she would curl up in the evenings once she'd got her mum to bed. Books were her friends. Books supplied refuge. Books took her away to other corners of the world.

It was odd, then, that for once she didn't want to wrap herself in their solitude. She wanted company, and not just the company of fictional characters. Today she wanted someone to listen to the worries in her life.

Everything is going to be okay. The silence in her room was the most deafening sound in the world when all that was in her head were false reassurances.

What if it wasn't okay?

Shoving aside the thought, she needed to check her wound was healing properly. As she glanced down, she wished the dressing they'd put in place was big enough to cover her unfurled nipple as well as the stitches. Not wanting to dwell on its worsening appearance, she quickly changed into cosy checked pyjamas and got into bed early. The champagne was making her drowsier than usual. It was a nice feeling. She'd not felt sleepy for days, the worry of life mounting on top of her, inducing her adrenaline and keeping her wide awake.

Perhaps she should make a few modifications to her room. A TV, for starters, with a mini fridge filled with her new favourite drink: champers. It would add a little more entertainment to the evenings.

When she went to plug her phone in to charge, she noticed the messages from Nathan. The first was a few hours old: *Been admitted to the hospital. But I'm not dead. So, that's something. How are you?*

The second was only half an hour old: *Can you drive? I need a lift tomorrow. I'm hoping you'll be able to come to my rescue.*

The moment of feeling sorry for herself ebbed away as she sat and read the messages again. What had happened to land him in hospital? She didn't like to think. This was one of those occasions when a message wouldn't cover it, so she rang his number instead. Clearly the last vapours of champagne lingering in her veins were making her far braver than usual. As she was very quickly learning, she was only going to live once, so there was no point in hesitating over phoning a gorgeous man when the chance came along. Screw never.

Chapter Nine

Day Seven

Nathan

Considering Nathan had thought he was dying, he should be pretty pleased with the discharge slip he now had in his hands. But the diagnosis on the form was putting it all into perspective. It hadn't been the heart attack or stroke he'd suspected. Not even anything potentially cancer-related or life-threatening. It had been, of all things, a panic attack.

Practically every medical professional he'd come into contact with had commented on how lucky he was that he'd passed out in the plane rather than mid-jump. Nathan gulped at the knowledge of what they meant. That would have been an altogether different sort of discharge form.

The problem was he didn't feel lucky. He wouldn't have believed he would be prone to experiencing panic attacks. He was brave. Courageous. Daring. A daredevil. So the diagnosis was completely at odds with the person he was. Or at least the person he'd *thought* he was.

That was why there was only one person Nathan wanted to contact when they said he needed someone to accompany him on his journey home. And it was a surprise even to him that she was the only one he was comfortable enough to ask. It had been a relief when she'd called him last night and a comfort knowing she was on her way to pick him up from the hospital.

It wasn't like he had the usual family set-up to fall back on. His mother was deceased, his father was AWOL and his half-brother was a waste of space. He'd not exactly had a traditional upbringing. He'd been lucky to have his grandparents as his main caregivers, but since they'd passed, his remaining family was next to useless. None of them would be worried that he'd landed up in hospital, no matter what the diagnosis was.

'Are you okay?' Emma asked once she'd arrived and he'd made no effort to move despite the nursing staff telling him he was free to go.

Nathan briefly glanced at the discharge note again. It made the pressure on his shoulders transform into a weight he'd never experienced before. Of all the things he'd thought might end up slowing him down, fear wasn't one of them. That was the thing that impelled him. At times it had driven him to the edge of destruction, but never had it stopped him in his tracks.

'You don't look okay,' Emma said when he didn't respond. She appeared entirely ill at ease.

Nathan felt bad for calling her when she had enough on her plate. There were plenty of friends he could have rung to pick him up without giving a full explanation of what was wrong. He'd certainly pranged himself enough times for any number of excuses to be plausible. He could have easily pleaded mild concussion as a reason to need an escort home. He should have called Tim and Leanne.

'I'm losing it.' It was possible he didn't know Emma well enough to be making such confessions, but it needed to be said and he needed to start somewhere.

'Oh.'

Nathan didn't know how to explain. He just passed her the form so she could read it for herself. Emma's glasses hid chestnut-brown eyes that reminded him of Bambi.

After studying the piece of paper, Emma's Bambi eyes took him in and she did the one thing he wasn't expecting. She opened her arms and held him in a hug.

'You know I don't have a car, don't you?'

Before the embrace even started, it was over. Despite its brevity, it made him feel marginally better about life. Perhaps he had called the right person after all, even though they were practically strangers. They were just two people with lumps.

'But you said you can drive?'

'Just because I have a driving licence doesn't mean I have a car.'

'So how are you giving me a lift home?'

'You only said you needed an escort. We're catching the bus.'

Nathan smiled. 'That wasn't quite what I was imagining, but thank you for coming to my rescue.' He'd been about to list the reasons they shouldn't catch a bus, but then realised he didn't really have any. Just because he hadn't been on one since he'd passed his driving test at seventeen, it didn't mean it wasn't a viable transport option. 'I think I might have forgotten how to use them.'

'I'm not asking you to drive it.'

There was something so pragmatic about Emma that the comment made Nathan laugh.

'I don't think anyone would trust me to drive it.'

Emma's serious expression turned into a cheeky grin, and for a fleeting moment he imagined her without her glasses and with her hair down. For a second, he was somewhere else entirely. Wow. Nathan shook his head. Where did that come from?

'Come on,' she said, that playful smirk still in action. 'We'll miss the next one if we hang around here too long.'

He followed Emma with a new sense of purpose, although that was fairly hard when he didn't have a clue where the bus stop was. He was fully reliant on her directions to get them where they needed to be.

'Why do you think it happened then?' Emma asked once they were outside the hospital.

'It's embarrassing.'

'I'm going to point out that this week I had you, a virtual stranger, hold my hand while a doctor squished my boob in the right direction to get a tissue sample. That's pretty high on the chart of embarrassing things, so you *have* to tell me. Whether you want to or not.'

To be fair, he had to tell someone, and she was the only person he was prepared to turn to. 'I can't believe I had a panic attack. I honestly thought I was going to die. It felt like I was having a heart attack – it was so hard to breathe. The last thing I remember is being on the plane and wondering if this is how it all ends. Apparently I passed out at that point. The next thing I remember is the plane going in to land with an ambulance waiting on the ground.'

'Sorry, I think I'm missing something. Which bit was embarrassing?' Emma stopped as they reached the bus shelter.

Nathan had thought it would be obvious. 'Well, it wasn't a heart attack, was it?'

'No, but you shouldn't be embarrassed by it. What do you think set it off?'

'I'm not sure. I'm not really the kind of guy who expects to end up having a panic attack.' He wasn't sure he'd believe it himself if it wasn't for the piece of paper now in his pocket.

'I don't think anyone ever expects to have one. It's not happened before then?'

'Never. It's not the kind of thing someone in my line of work can have going on.'

'So do you know what caused it?'

Nathan hadn't thought about it – hadn't really *wanted* to think about it – but as soon as Emma asked the question, he knew what the answer was. The realisation winded him.

'It's the not knowing, isn't it?' Emma said it before he was able to.

Nathan took a deep breath. 'It's stupid, but I can't stop thinking about it.'

A bus pulled into the stop. Emma signalled for them to go over. It turned out buses hadn't changed much in the decade since his school days, when he'd last got on one. The only difference was Emma had a fancy card that she had to scan, whereas he had to pay.

'It's not stupid,' Emma said. 'I've thought about nothing else all week. I haven't been eating properly, I've been so worried. It's just so monumental. It has the potential to change everything.' They settled onto a seat at the back of the bus, away from any other passengers.

It really did, when he thought about it. But he'd known about this for so long. He hadn't expected to react this way when the moment finally came. 'Can I tell you something that's going to sound really stupid?'

'Go on.'

'I've always thought I was going to die aged twenty-seven. I've always had this recurring dream that this is the year when it all ends. So, when I found the lump, it wasn't a surprise.' It was the first time he'd admitted the dream out loud to another person.

'Well, that's different. But I don't plan to die at twenty-seven, so you can't either.' A fold appeared between Emma's eyebrows. 'You can't honestly believe a dream has predicted your future?' She peered over her glasses at him, looking every inch the librarian she was.

'I know. It sounds crackers, but I've had it that frequently I've always thought it was true. The problem is, because I've always thought I know when I'm going to die, I thought I would be ready for it. Like it would be some kind of homecoming. For my whole life, death has never scared me, and yet suddenly it's within reaching distance and I'm petrified.'

'That's certainly a way to stockpile your conviction. You won't believe you're going to live if you think like that. It might still be nothing. Your statistical odds are far better than mine. Thoughts like that will stop you from fighting before you've even started.'

The bus pulled over at a stop before trundling off on its way again.

Emma was right, but it was going to be a hard mindset for Nathan to shift given the constant reminders his subconscious liked to provide him with. 'It might be nothing, but I can't shake the feeling it definitely is cancer. That my dream has been trying to tell me something.'

'And if you're anything like me, you're counting the minutes until you find out.'

'When do you find out?' Nathan had never known time to go so slowly – usually his life whizzed past – but he realised he was being selfish, worrying about his own imminent death when Emma was facing exactly the same prospect.

'Next week. And it can't come soon enough. I might end up doing something else silly if I'm not careful. I know it's the reason I walked out of work.'

'Maybe work didn't deserve you if you were that happy to walk out.'

'Yeah, maybe. I just can't afford to not go in.'

'So did you go back with your tail between your legs?'

'No. I called in sick. I'm not going to go back until I have the results. My arsehole boss might be a bit more sympathetic if it turns out I have the big C.'

Nathan laughed inappropriately. 'Sorry, it's just I didn't expect you to swear. You don't seem the type.' Not that he was even sure what he meant by that. She just seemed like the kind of calm person who tended to be super polite all the time.

'Believe me, if there is anyone in the world who deserves to be called names, it's Trevor.'

'He sounds delightful. I'll have to pop into the library just to see what you're having to put up with. Not that I know where the library is.' Nathan took note of their surroundings. 'And where are we anyway?'

'We get off in a couple of stops.'

'I hope you're not going out of your way to get me home?'

'I've had to move a few things about, but it's okay, because it turns out you're two streets away from me. There's only one stop difference and it'll be a quick walk for me to get back.'

They arrived at the right stop and got off the bus. Nathan admired how different the scenery was when his gaze wasn't stuck on the road. The bus journey hadn't been so bad, especially with Emma keeping him company.

'Well, thank you for getting me out of the hospital. I didn't really want to involve anyone else.' His friends would have asked for more details than he was willing to share.

'I'm walking you all the way home,' Emma insisted. 'So, you still haven't told anyone yet?'

'No. Like you said, it might be nothing. I don't want to worry anyone unnecessarily. What about you?'

'Me neither. I don't want to think about what's going to happen if it is. I plan on living in happy denial for a while longer.'

'Look, it's still early… Do you want to do something?' It was only half three and he could do without sitting at home alone while both his housemates were still at work.

Emma checked her watch. 'I'd love to, but I need to be back by half four to sort my mum's dinner out. Sorry, it's a bit of a bind, but she can't do it herself.'

'But we have an hour.'

'Yeah, but it's not really long enough to do anything, is it? There's nothing to do round here.'

'Hold up.' Nathan stopped quickly to turn and face Emma, nearly sending her off balance. 'Never are we wasting another hour.

An hour is sacred. An hour could open up a universe. An hour could change the world.'

'Oh-kaaay. So what are we doing with this hour?'

'I haven't worked that out yet.' He should have probably come up with something before starting his speech.

Emma flashed her cute semi-grin. 'Definitely sounds life-changing.'

'I know.' Inspiration suddenly hit him. 'You need to cook for your mum, right?'

'Yes.'

'So, how about we have a barbeque? I can cook for you both and you can have a night off for once. I keep meaning to have one but haven't got round to it. We just need to go buy the food and we can grab my portable barbeque from my house. Sound like a plan?'

'But it's February!'

'So?'

Emma turned her head, obviously looking in the direction of her home. 'I'm not sure. My mum needs a lot of help. She might not be comfortable with a stranger around while she's eating.'

'If that's the case, I can cook and go. I don't have to stay.' Nathan moved nearer to catch her attention again. She was still staring in the opposite direction. When she didn't turn back, he tried one last time. 'It's just a chance to not waste an hour, and to distract us both from the fact time is moving appallingly slowly while we're waiting to find out exactly what we're facing.'

At last Emma returned her attention to him, as if she'd found her way back into the room. 'We're going to have a barbeque in February so we don't waste an hour of our lives?'

'Pretty much.' Nathan nodded.

'You're nuts.'

'It's been said before.'

Emma extended her hand. 'You're on.'

They shook on it. 'To never wasting an hour.' And all of a sudden, Nathan wanted to be holding a lot more than just her hand.

Chapter Ten

Emma

The thought of never wasting an hour was making Emma think she'd lost too many already. As they headed to the shop for supplies, a realisation came to her... Life wasn't what she'd expected it to be. It didn't mean that she wasn't content, but like everyone, she hadn't been aware of her future story. Being a carer wasn't what she'd dreamed of being bound to as she'd grown. She'd dreamed of owning a quaint cottage and running her own mobile library. She'd dreamed of something that was far closer to independence.

'What would you do, if you knew you could only do one more thing? What would be your last thing?' she asked, hoping that heading to the local supermarket for sausages didn't end up being her last thing. Not that planning a barbeque for her mum wasn't a nice thing to be doing – her mum would love it, even if it was going to be without the benefit of sunshine.

'That's a big question. I thought we were trying to distract ourselves from our life predicaments. Shouldn't we be sticking with things like whether lettuce or onion will be our token burger vegetable of choice?'

Emma glanced at him. Nathan was wearing a plain white T-shirt and shorts. Nobody who'd just been discharged from hospital should look that good in a plain T-shirt or be wearing something so seasonally inappropriate. She had to remind herself to pay attention to what he was saying, not what he was wearing. 'No question – fried onions are a barbeque essential. And I didn't mean it in a morbid way. I'm realising that I spend far too much of life just… getting on. I do things in order for life to function, not necessarily because they're the things I want to do.'

'I think you're asking the wrong person.' Nathan grabbed a basket once they were through the automatic doors.

'Why? You're the never-waste-an-hour guy.'

'Because I've spent my life pretending that everything was the last thing I was ever going to do. And I've got no closer to discovering the meaning of life as a result. I'm not even sure if I can remember all the things that should be on a barbeque shopping list. Right, what do we need?'

They bounced about the aisles collecting all the burgers, sausages, bread rolls, relish and salad they'd need to create a decent barbeque. Nathan was a ball of energy catapulting from one display to the next. It was like spending time with a five-year-old and feeling instantly worn out from their level of enthusiasm for life. If there was a pill for Nathan's outlook on life, Emma wanted to take one.

Watching Nathan, Emma realised the answer to her own question and it stopped her in her tracks. 'I'm not sure if my answer is valid.'

'The answer to what?'

'What's the last thing I'd do if I could choose *anything*? It seems so selfish to say it, but I'd love to spend a day with my mum from ten years ago. Before things got so bad.' Emma loved her mother no matter what, but she missed the freedom of just being, of doing things without thought. She'd love a single day of that feeling.

'I get that. I'd love to spend a day with my mum. She died when I was young.'

Emma instantly recognised her faux pas. Her mum might not be the version of herself that she once was, but she was still in Emma's life and a firm fixture in her daily routine. Her father had left when she was seven, but at least she had the ability to call him if she ever wanted to. She was lucky. 'God, I'm *so* sorry. I should have realised. When did it happen?' Finding the right words was proving to be beyond her capabilities.

'The day I was born. So an entire day with her truly would be beyond anything I've ever experienced before.'

Nathan picked up a tin of sweetcorn before returning it to the shelf and heading towards the chilled section.

Emma followed. 'My goodness. I'm so sorry. I don't even know what to say.' She lived in fear of losing her mum, and her heart ached as she watched her mother fade, but she couldn't imagine having not had her in her life. It was an impossibility.

'You don't need to say anything. I was fortunate to have grandparents that were sprightly enough to keep up with me until they passed.' Nathan caught her eye and placed an arm around her shoulders.

Emma was pretty sure it was an act of reassurance. She should be the one dishing those out, seeing as she was the one digging holes. 'I'm so sorry. I can't even begin to imagine. Was your dad ever about?'

'He's never been very reliable. He reacted badly to my mum's death and took off. He had a string of relationships afterwards. I ended up with a half-brother, Marcus, out of one of them, but my dad never had much to do with me. It was decided very early on that I would live with my mother's parents. It was a long time ago now, but even then I knew I was better off with them. Anyway, enough about me. Being that all the things we've wished for so far won't ever come true, what is it you'd actually do? What one last thing would you do if it were humanly possible?'

Nathan was moving the subject on, and who wouldn't with that history of loss? She wanted to find the place where all that hurt existed and dish out a hug. But they were in a supermarket, with a security guard trailing them for something to do. The window closed quicker than it had opened when Nathan moved his arm from her shoulders.

Emma thought back to the question. The one experience she'd missed out on so far made her blush. She fumbled for another suggestion. 'I guess it would have to be a break from the routine. I don't feel like I've done enough adventurous things with my life. I'd love to go on a road trip, but it's the kind of thing I'm not sure I'd ever get around to doing.'

'Where are we driving to first?' Nathan asked, as if they were about to go off and do it instead of filling the shopping basket with bread rolls and burgers.

Emma stopped to imagine for a minute. She landed on a place where nothing else existed. Where there were no concerns about what she needed to do next. 'Puffins. We're going to head off to see puffins.' She'd always wanted to see one in the wild, ever since she was a little girl. It stemmed from her obsession with books. The small bird was the emblem of some of her first childhood reads. Often, in the same way people liked to sniff the pages of books, she would stroke her fingers along the spine, curious about the bird as much as the title printed on the side.

'Bit random, but hey! Puffins it is. First stop barbeque… Next stop puffins.'

Emma's laughter trilled through the air with a lightness she wasn't feeling. If only it were that easy. She could never abandon her mum like that. It was just the way things were. 'You haven't answered the question yet. What would you do, if it was the last thing you were ever going to do? If you've lived with that philosophy at heart, surely it gives you a better idea over what would be the *best* last thing to do?'

'That's easy to answer. It's just not that simple to action.'

It sounded like they were both in the same boat once again. 'What isn't?'

'This recent breasts-with-issues business has made me realise how selfish I've been all my life. I may have been living for the moment, but everything I've done has been for my own personal enjoyment and satisfaction. The problem with that is it's only ever been fleeting. I might have done the things that set my soul on fire, but what happens once the flames go out? How do you ever keep it going? It's made me realise that, if I were going to do anything as a last act, I'd want it to be fundraising or something for a good cause. Something real. Something lasting.'

Emma found the right kind of plastic cheese slices and added them to the basket. 'Don't you jump with people who are fundraising for charity all the time? You must have raised hundreds of pounds through your job.'

'I hate to admit it, but I wouldn't be there if I wasn't getting paid for it. I'm there purely for the thrills and the money, not because I'm strapped to someone hoping to raise funds for charity.'

'It still counts though. You might think it's selfish, but really you're doing something incredible.' There was nothing Nathan had done since she met him that would make her consider him a selfish person.

'I'm not sure about that. I just know I'd like to do something more. Make my mark, you know?'

'Any idea what you'd do?'

Having navigated every aisle within the supermarket, Nathan started to scan their items through the self-checkout.

'That's the part I'm not sure about. If I asked my mates to sponsor me on a skydive they'd laugh at me, but then what can I do that's bigger than jumping out of a plane?'

Emma pondered for a moment as Nathan did an efficient job of sorting their shopping. 'What about running a marathon, or one of those mud courses?'

'I really admire anyone who takes part in those, but I want to do something different, and I don't mean by running in a chicken suit. If we are truly on about our last acts, then it needs to be epic.'

'Don't say that! Last acts sounds so… final. How about we call them everlasting acts?' It was scary. Emma wondered whether she should have even started to think about what might be to come. Because when it came down to it, everyone was scared. There was always something bigger to tackle. There was always a fight to be had, a battle to win, a love to get over. Neither of them knew what it was they would be facing.

'It's an improvement on calling it a bucket list. Everlasting acts sounds better to me. But right at this moment, we just need to concentrate on never wasting an hour. Shall we?' Nathan extended his hand out for her.

Without any need for further explanation, Emma knew exactly what to do. Their shopping was still piled up at the checkout, but ignoring that, she allowed herself to be waltzed around the aisle like they were a couple without a care in the world. Never wasting an hour should definitely involve dancing in the aisles with strangers looking at them oddly.

It was like there was music playing, even though there was none. The beeping of the tills, the trolleys sweeping over tiles, the buzzing of the fridges – all in tune with their rhythm. In their movements, to an imaginary beat, there was a certain magic to be found. The air shifted as they twirled. And in that dance, it was if a wave of realisation was dawning. What if, in all this madness, they were going to save each other? As she thought it, she felt it – a curious certainty they were meant to be in each other's life.

It was a new feeling, being this close to a man. If she were able to store this moment in a glass jar, she would treasure the sensation of his chest moving as it was pressed against hers. She would keep hold of the shiver that passed through her when his breath reached her neck. She hadn't known this man for very long, but somehow they were meant to be here, pressed together, as they laughed and danced and lived.

And as every bystander in the shop glared at this display of revelry that was far too jovial for the time of day, Emma's weirdo stranger friend went to kiss her.

It was a fraction of a moment. And for a fraction of a moment Emma wanted to respond. She wanted to kiss him like it was the only way two souls were able to connect. Some confirmation that, whatever this sense of belonging was, at the very least she wasn't imagining it.

'I hope you two dancing queens are planning on paying for those?' the none-too-happy security guard asked.

It was alarming, how quickly the world could shift. How swiftly magic could be sucked out of the air. How soon after a moment it was possible to question if it had even existed.

Whatever tempo had been there was gone. And like a dandelion seed blown away on the wind, Emma knew there was no hope, and not much point in trying to catch it.

Chapter Eleven

Nathan

Nathan's place, as he'd expected, was empty when he went in to retrieve his barbeque. There might have been two other people in his house share, but they rarely saw each other, what with them all being hard at work and hard at socialising. Truly, it was just a place to lay their heads before the next adventure.

It wasn't until the past couple of weeks that he'd realised what an empty kind of existence it was. It wasn't that he didn't have friends – he had plenty. But who could he call on when the chips were really down? What did he have to show for his life of excess? Not nearly as much as he'd like. The question Emma posed had him thinking – what would be left of him when he was gone? He didn't have a clue how to perform an 'everlasting act', but he knew he had to try. But right now he was going to settle for doing something for someone other than himself. Cooking dinner for a stranger seemed like a pretty good start.

He wasn't going to think about wanting to kiss Emma. It wasn't like he hadn't experienced the instinct before. Kissing was part of the curriculum for living like there was no tomorrow. But smooching on impulse had been known to get him in trouble. That wasn't what he wanted with Emma. There were all sorts of other battles they would have to face without that getting in the way. There was no going back if he kissed her. There was just one set of automatic doors between the life before and the life after.

He wanted to stay on this side of that set of doors. The side that was known and uncomplicated. But would he be able to describe anything as uncomplicated ever again?

He grabbed the barbeque and attempted to concentrate on the present. He had enough preconceptions of the future to not want to dwell on that for a moment.

Chapter Twelve

Emma

Emma fumbled with her key in the lock. It was a telltale sign that, despite trying to play it cool, she was not achieving it in the slightest. Nathan, who was going round the side passage with their barbeque haul, had gone to kiss her. Kiss *her*. On *her* lips.

Once she'd managed to negotiate her way through the doorway, she had to take a moment to try and calm down. Because the thing was, he hadn't kissed her. He might have thought about it briefly, but he'd stopped himself. That moment was gone. So she needed to concentrate on getting through this meal – not thinking about his mouth or the smell of his shampoo or how nice it had felt being pressed to his torso or the fact that she'd never been kissed before.

'Emma, is that you? Are you okay?'

It was unusual for Emma to hesitate in going to say hello to her mum. She dusted her work shirt, brushing off invisible traces of the things that hadn't been. She'd not mentioned that she wasn't planning on going in for the immediate future, so she'd worn it as if she were off to work as usual that morning. There were so many things she wasn't currently mentioning to her mum.

'Fine, Mum. I've just got some chewing gum stuck on my shoe. I'll be in in a minute.' Emma didn't know where that had come from. There was nothing on her shoe and yet the little lie had fallen from her lips so easily. How many more would follow?

Making sure she was presentable, unable to do anything about the flush in her cheeks, Emma went into the confines of her mother's living space.

'You're late, love. Everything okay?'

Emma was such a creature of habit that it was glaringly obvious when anything was out of sync. She hadn't even realised that she was later than she normally would be.

'Er, yeah, fine.'

Her mum was tipped over slightly in her chair, not quite where she should be and obviously unable to right herself. Guilt over not returning sooner pricked Emma's conscience as she adjusted her mum's position.

'Did you have a good day, love?'

'You should have rung me, Mum, and asked me to come back earlier.' The phone was voice-activated, in case her mother was ever in a position where she couldn't reach it, and failing that, there was an emergency cord around her neck.

'Oh, it's no bother. It only just happened.'

Not so long ago, her mum's nerves had been intact enough to allow her muscles to correct her posture. That wasn't the case any more. The MS was eating away at the lining of her nerves, making it impossible for the signals to get through. It was cruel how a disease was able to chip away at a person.

'You need to let me know, Mum. Please. We don't want you having any more problems with your skin.' It had taken weeks for a small ulcer to heal before Christmas. They didn't need any more hiccups like that, especially if Emma wasn't going to be in a position to help.

'Duly noted.' Carole smiled, giving a shaky salute towards her daughter's bossiness.

'I'm not joking.'

'I know, love. I just…' Carole's voice trailed off, as if any remaining gusto had been punched out of her.

Emma chastised herself. It was so easy to get concerned. To forget how hard it must be, living in the confines of this room. The last thing her mother needed was her coming along and pointing out her shortfalls. And right at this moment, it wasn't about that. They were supposed to be having an afternoon of spontaneous fun.

'I'm sorry.' Emma fussed over her mother's position a bit more. 'I have a surprise for you.' She smiled, trying to ease into the idea that Nathan was busy cooking outside while she was tending to her mum.

'Have you brought eclairs?'

They were her favourite, and Emma was in the habit of getting them as a treat, even if it did end up being a messy affair. 'Better.'

'I think you'd have a hard time beating an eclair. What is it?'

'You mean *who* is it.'

Her mother's grin reappeared. 'Have we got a guest?'

'Sort of. We have a chef!'

'Really? Who?' Carole jerked more markedly with the news. 'It's never your brother?'

Emma almost laughed at the thought. She was quite right… It would never be her brother. James didn't know the first thing about being helpful, let alone ever having the good grace to show up and help them out with dinner. 'Sorry, I didn't realise you fancied burnt frozen pizza, or I'd have called him!' Her brother had been a notoriously bad cook during his teen years, massacring the simplest of foods.

'No, of course not.' There was disappointment traipsing the edges of her mum's words. The empty hope that never lifted. A mother's love that never died.

'The chef is Nathan. Although he's not an actual chef. But he did offer to cook us a barbeque.' Emma hoped her mother wouldn't ask too many questions. Especially when she didn't have the answers prepared. She wasn't sure how she was going to explain Nathan and his presence.

'A barbeque?' The delight on her mum's face was worth any white lies she might have to tell between now and burger-in-a-bun time.

'Yep.'

'Isn't it too cold?'

'Not according to Nathan.' Just saying his name made her smile, sending a thrill through her in ways she'd not been aware were possible. She didn't want to like him in that way, as she knew it would make their whole situation messier, but her instincts said something different. 'I don't think he's too worried about categorising seasons. He's wearing shorts,' Emma added, to clarify just how at odds he was with the cold compared to every other person in Wiltshire.

'As long as we don't have to wear any!' Her mum smiled, apparently not at all fazed by the fact that a complete stranger had turned up at the house.

'I'll go and see how things are getting on.'

'Okay, love. But I want to see this barbequing in action, so don't leave me here.'

'I'll be back soon. Promise.'

Emma left the lounge, and as she made her way through the kitchen, she worried for a moment that Nathan wouldn't be there. That perhaps this was some mirage she'd been imagining. A handsome man, who'd almost kissed her, was cooking dinner for her and her mother. It didn't sound like the kind of thing that usually happened in her life. She'd been spending far too long with her head buried in books, feeding herself ideas that were far beyond the scope of reality.

But as she reached the garden, here was that fantasy: tall, dark, handsome *and* capable. If the ruffled hair and designer stubble weren't enough to make her weak at the knees, then his tanned features and broad shoulders were. He was humming to some music coming from his phone.

Emma recognised the tune. 'Smashing Pumpkins,' she said, without thinking.

'Yeah, do you know it?'

'"Farewell and Goodnight". One of my favourites.' It was ironic that they both liked a song that referenced enjoying every hour of every day. At least that was how Emma interpreted the words, along with its sense of being a goodbye…

They both nodded to this shared love and listened to the melody as it played out. The lyrics had a bittersweet meaning when she tuned into them. Often, when she heard this song, she would think about her mother, but now it brought renewed meaning as she started to think of how the goodnight song might be her own. There was a swell in her chest. Her emotions hadn't been this all over the shop since she was a teenager brewing chin-spots. She peered at the clouds to check if the skies were opening, but even though they were grey and plentiful, she was the only thing spilling over with the waterworks. She subtly wiped away the wayward tear.

'I'm going to switch to something more upbeat.' A *High School Musical* track started pumping from Nathan's phone.

'Really?'

'You can't beat a good musical song to help bring out the happy.' Nathan beamed at her and started to snap his tongs to the beat. 'Come on. Don't tell me you don't love this?'

Emma didn't want to openly admit to loving the song, partly due to a crush on Zac Efron. Come to think of it, Nathan had a bit of Efron about him as he swaggered some dodgy dance moves in his shorts and the thick Barbour-style gilet he'd picked up along with the barbeque. The cold February day meant he needed the extra layer.

'Mum is quite happy about you being here.' Emma returned her focus to why they were here. It wasn't to re-enact a movie scene; it was to create one of their own for the benefit of her mother.

'Has she asked any questions?'

'Not yet.' Emma hesitated and decided to reemphasise the fact that she didn't want her mother to know that she was being screened for cancer. 'Can we not mention how we met?'

'Not a word. I think we should say we travel on the same bus and we started talking because we get off at the same stop.'

It wasn't the biggest lie in the world. They did get the bus today and they did get off at the same stop. It wouldn't take much to elaborate, making out that they'd discovered they were near neighbours over a few journeys. 'I can go with that,' Emma said, glad they'd agreed some kind of plan.

But it didn't take away from her concerns regarding how introducing someone new to her mother would go. She hadn't realised it would feel like a problem until today. After all, she was always introducing her mum to new people: district nurses, lunchtime carers, staff from the day centre she visited once a week. It wasn't like their life was entirely isolated, but they were all health care professionals who knew about her mother's illness and the extent to which it affected her life. She didn't have to think about what she needed to tell them when they had a set of case notes to refer to.

'I'll go and set up the dining table. Do you want to eat inside with us?' Emma was hesitating too much. Letting her thoughts take over the actual living part of living.

'If that's cool?'

Emma nodded. It was cool, even if it wasn't. She was the one that needed to get over her mental hurdles. She took one last glimpse at Nathan as she went back inside. It would seem that even in the darkest of moments, life was sometimes able to provide light.

As always, Emma laid out the protective cover for the floor and got the specialist cutlery and cup her mother would need.

'It smells delicious,' Carole shouted from the lounge.

'Can you smell it all the way in there?' Emma went to retrieve her mother, taking the brakes off her wheelchair and manoeuvring her through the house. They were waiting for a specialist electric wheelchair that would be suitable for navigating through the house, but it seemed like any such equipment required jumping through several hoops and twenty-eight meetings in order to access it.

'What's on the menu?' Carole asked as Emma managed to steer her round the difficult corner between the lounge and kitchen.

'Burgers, mostly. And sausages, if they aren't charcoal. I just need to get the rest of the food ready.'

Rather than place her mum next to the table, she faced her towards the old-fashioned open kitchen so they could talk while Emma put salad and crisps into bowls and prepped rolls.

'Can I go outside? I'd like to see the barbequing in action.'

'Of course. I'll just finish here and then we'll get you sorted.' What a simple request. And yet how complicated it seemed. Buttering the last of the buns, she attempted to push her reluctant thoughts aside.

She grabbed her mum's coat and some extra blankets. It wasn't the nicest of days and she wanted to make sure she'd be warm enough. Nathan might be oblivious to the elements, but that didn't mean the rest of the world were able to behave with such disregard. The last thing she needed was her mother getting poorly.

'It's cold out there. Are you sure you want to go out?' Emma wasn't able to stop herself from trying to discourage her mum. Even though, right at this moment, it was supposed to be about embracing the hour, there was an impulse to prevent the worst that she wasn't able to put to bed. The thought of her mum getting ill was causing a domino effect in her head. There was already so much to deal with. Something like that on top of everything else might be the thing to make it all fall down.

'Of course I'm sure. I could do with some cold air in my lungs.'

It wasn't the cold air that was worrying Emma. It was all the bacteria that lingered unseen. New forms her mum hadn't experienced yet. Tiny germs that somehow had the capacity to change the course of life entirely.

Emma stopped herself mid thought and zipped up her mum's coat. When had she got so hyper-cautious?

She knew it was because of the pending biopsy results. They were making her worry about everything, more than she ever had before. Little things were becoming great chasms that she wasn't able to overcome.

She needed to snap out of it. She needed to focus on everlasting acts, not temporary anxieties.

Emma got the portable ramps out for the back steps. They weren't particularly heavy, just cumbersome to move about. The real trick was making sure they were in the right place. Getting them in exactly the correct position made moving the wheelchair outside a whole lot easier.

With those in place, Emma went and got her mum. She always went on the ramp in reverse to make the whole procedure easier. That way, if anything was in the wrong place, it meant at least she was in the right position to fix the situation. It only took one almost-making-your-mother-nosedive-into-the-garden moment for her to learn this was the better way to go about things.

It was after she'd started the manoeuvre that she remembered she wasn't really supposed to be doing any manual handling on this scale. Her side pinched and she took a sharp breath on the pain inching through to her ribs.

'Let me!' Nathan gave Emma an earnest look.

'Thank you,' she said, realising that she was trying to carry on far too vehemently as if nothing was wrong.

'A gentleman as well as a chef. How come I've never heard of you before, Nathan?' Emma's mum was doing her best to get a peek, even though Nathan was behind her.

If Emma hadn't been busy tending to the pain she'd caused herself, she would have been straight in with an answer. She had no idea what her answer would have been, but it seemed fair to be the one to field any questions.

'I'm a man of many talents. I do hope you like burnt sausages.' Nathan moved the wheelchair with ease and swung it round so her mother had a prime view of the smoking barbeque and not Emma rubbing her side.

'I'll take any sausage action I can get.'

'Mum!' Emma had to say something. She may be a woman approaching her thirties – or at least hoping to – but she wasn't beyond being embarrassed by her mother.

'So how do you two know each other?' Carole attempted to look towards her, but her position wouldn't let her so she settled her gaze on Nathan.

Emma didn't move to be in her mum's sightline. She was still in too much pain for that. It was clear Carole was hoping that at long last she was about to be introduced to a boyfriend.

'We met at the bus stop. My usual mode of transport is temporarily out of action and Emma's been helping me get to grips with being on a bus for the first time in ten years. Have you got a plate I can bung these sausages on, Emma? They're pretty much done.'

'I'll go grab one.'

It was with record speed that Emma found a plate, grabbing two to spare herself a second journey if another was needed. She didn't want to miss out on any of what was being said. Seeing as Nathan's tale of how they'd met was a ruse, it would help if she knew exactly what her mum had been told.

Emma almost dropped the plate when she rejoined them. Nathan had moved the chair so her mum was able to have a go at flipping burgers. Emma's predicted health and safety assessment produced such terrifying results that she almost instinctively threw a plate at Nathan's head. What was he thinking?

She hadn't been clear enough about her mum's illness and the problems it caused. How was Nathan to know that the lack of control she possessed over her own muscles was likely to result in her burning herself, or a burger flying into his face? But as she headed over in slow motion, she wasn't quick enough to stop what was happening.

With Nathan's assistance, the palette knife slid under a sizzling burger, and between them, despite the occasional tremor, they flipped it. And her mum laughed for the first time in a long while. A laugh that tinkled through the air like it was lighter than life itself; a molecule escaping into the atmosphere saying, 'I lived and I lived well.'

One moment it was there. The next it was lost.

Emma wanted to grab it. To make that molecule stay put. She needed to keep it in her pocket as a reminder that not everything ended up as badly as she thought it might. That strangers could become friends who were kind enough to gift an hour and make her mother laugh.

She needed to remember that not everything was designed to make life difficult. Okay, there were difficulties, but that shouldn't stop moments like this existing.

And yet, despite the bauble of laughter still hanging in the air, she couldn't stop herself from asking the question. 'Are you okay, Mum?'

'Absolutely.' Carole smiled as she turned to her. 'You never told me you knew a skydiving instructor?'

Nathan had taken over flipping duties now and Emma relaxed again.

'We've not known each other that long.'

'I'd love to do that. I've always wanted to jump out of a plane and float back to the earth.' There was colour in her mum's cheeks as she confessed to the desire.

'Have you? You've never told me.' Emma was surprised to hear this revelation when her own response to the thought of jumping out of a plane was to keep her feet firmly planted on the ground.

'Why don't you? You'd love it,' Nathan chipped in. He made sure Carole was comfortably seated again before starting to place sausages and burgers onto a plate.

Carole looked down and took her own figure in. 'It's not exactly something I've ever imagined would be possible.'

'I don't see why not. I'm sure I could get something sorted. Burger, anyone?'

All at once the molecule popped. Emma heard it. Because even though everyone else was still smiling, she wasn't able to. There was lightness around her, but she wasn't able to bring it towards the heaviness in her heart. She was never going to say it out loud, for fear her mother would hear the molecule burst too, but no, there wasn't one part of her that could imagine her mum jumping out of a plane.

Some days, however hard she tried to combat those thoughts, everything seemed to be against her and it became impossibly hard to see beyond the here and now.

Some days a barbeque in February had to be miracle enough.

Nathan's Diary

Respite is such a rare thing in life. The offering of a blank page is no longer an option. We are rushing.

We are windswept.

We are fighting to be heard.

There is never enough silence.

The nights I have without dreams are so infrequent that when they occur the peacefulness of the morning is untold. What a blessing a blank page is. The opportunity to start anew.

Today isn't the day I die. Today is the day I start to make a difference.

Chapter Thirteen

Day Nine

Emma's life was made up of broken pieces. Nothing was neatly in place like it once had been. When Nathan had called saying he wanted to start making a difference, to begin putting his everlasting acts into place, taking him to the youth club had seemed like a good idea.

Thursday was her day off from the library. It was the day she played catch-up with chores and then, for an hour each week, she helped run the young carers' group. She took it in turns with her friend Alice to organise an activity for the kids. Providing them with the chance to be children was the part she enjoyed most. And it was great to have something else to focus on — she didn't have to fix a problem or finish a task. Their only job was to have fun. It seemed like exactly the kind of thing that Nathan needed to occupy him. It would do them both some good.

At the very least, some sense of normality would resume within her week. As she wasn't planning on returning to work just yet, continuing to volunteer at the carers' group would give her life some structure to hang off. It might also give Nathan some ideas about what he would be able to do to make a difference.

'I'm going to say you're here for a work placement. We sometimes have trainee social workers who pop along.'

'Where are we going? Is that the library?'

They were heading across a green to a single-storey white building.

'It's the community building. It's used for local groups, mostly. The youth group meet here weekly and the carers' group meets as part of the youth club evening.'

'And this is part of your work?'

'I do this voluntarily. Or rather, it's more a case of never having left. I used to come here as a youngster and I helped set up a young carers' group for this area. A decade later and I'm still here. Alice and I run it these days. We've got some great kids who come along. For some of them, it's the only time they meet others in the same position as them or get to enjoy an hour of being themselves.'

'Wow. So you manage to work, look after your mum and help run a carers' group? I think I need to up my game.'

'I only work part-time. And I love running the group. It's what gives me my sanity at times.' She wasn't sure it was so virtuous if she got as much out of it as she put in.

'But still… Some people wouldn't find the energy for something like this with everything that you do elsewhere. Believe me, I've spent far too many evenings lounging on the sofa.'

'I imagine jumping out of planes is quite tiring. I don't think anyone would say there is anything wrong with needing to rest.' Emma glanced across the grass as they strolled over. The first of the spring daisies were evident, the sight of them making her think of the seasons to come and whether she would get to see the white and yellow flowers push through the grass next year. She didn't want to think like that, though. Despite everything being out of place, she liked to live in the belief that everything happened for a reason. That, perhaps, the shift in the pattern of her life was occurring for a beneficial purpose.

'What about you? Your mum seems very keen to jump out of a plane. Isn't it something you want to do as well?'

Emma was quick to shake her head. 'I like to keep my feet well and truly planted on the ground.'

'We need to work out how to get you puffin-spotting instead.'

'That is far more my cup of tea,' Emma said, distracted as they reached the doors of the white building. However much coming here was a step towards normality, it also reminded her how much had changed. Would anything ever be the same again, with something so life-defining hanging on the peripheries of her life? 'My friend Alice doesn't know about… Well, you know.' Emma pointed towards her boobs.

'I wouldn't ever say a thing.' Nathan made a gesture indicating he was zipping his lips.

She wanted to tell Alice. She was her closest friend, after all. But in the same way she didn't want to worry her mother unnecessarily, she was taking the same stance with her friend. She would tell them the news if it turned out there was any. She took a deep breath, praying that wouldn't be the case. 'Alice has organised the activity this week. We take it in turns.' She pushed against the heavy doors and was greeted by the sound of teenagers working at making themselves heard. She loved that noise – every second full of energy, never dropping a beat. It was such a juxtaposition to her own quiet life and it always made her smile. She relished the time she spent here.

'This way.' Emma waved Nathan in the right direction. The young carers' group got to squirrel away in one of the side rooms off the main hall.

'Doesn't this make them feel like they're missing out, if they're not part of the main group?' Nathan was looking at the larger hall, where music was playing and various ball games were breaking out.

'It seems to have the opposite effect. It makes them feel special. They get to join the larger group after we've finished, and they always want to know what we've been up to this week. Of course, what they don't realise is that having the smaller group allows them to open up and talk about home life. If any of them have had a bad week they can talk about it in ways they wouldn't necessarily get the chance to if they went straight to the larger group. It kind of acts like a safe haven, being able to share with others in a similar predicament who they know won't judge. Not that the other kids here would, but there's just so much peer pressure from every quarter… It's just nice that, for a brief period of time, they get the chance for some kind of normality. It's something I really appreciated as a teen when I was coming here. To be honest, it's the reason I still come.'

'It sounds like you're doing a really good thing. For you and the kids.'

Emma pushed open the door into the smaller, calmer side room. 'Hey, Alice, we have a work experience guest joining us. I hope that's okay?'

Alice's beam said it was more than okay. Her smile wasn't usually that broad. It was clear that Emma's best friend wasn't oblivious to this man's good looks and charm.

The members of the youth group were already getting stuck into their project. Alice was always organised and had printed off instructions to help them all out.

'What's today's activity?' Nobody was far enough through the task for Emma to work out what the end product was going to be.

'We're doing some découpage. I asked them all to bring in a container they used regularly that they'd like to do up. I have some spares if you two would like to join in?'

'Why not?' Nathan said.

It was amazing, Nathan thought, how cutting up tiny pieces of wrapping paper decorated with some of his favourite action heroes was proving to be therapeutic. The kid he was sharing the paper with must have been about twelve.

'These look cool, huh?' Nathan said, attempting to strike up a bit of conversation.

The boy flicked his gaze towards him. It wasn't a look of disapproval. It wasn't a welcoming one either.

'What are you using yours for once it's done?' he tried again.

The kid gazed at him again. Longer this time, as if it would help suss him out. 'It's my dad's pill box.'

There were no amount of '*pow*' captions to lighten the blow of that. Of all the fun and frivolous things this young boy could be doing, he was instead decorating one of the hardest parts of his dad's life. Nathan held out his hand. 'Hi, I'm Nathan.'

If he was meeting someone braver than he was, it seemed right that he should at least put up a formal introduction.

'I'm Rudi. What are you going to use yours for?' Rudi shook his hand.

The box Nathan had been given was not much more than twenty centimetres cubed. 'I figure it'll be perfect for my work locker. I need somewhere to put everything from my pockets – all the stuff I'm not allowed to take with me when I'm jumping out of a plane.'

It might blow the cover story that he was here on work experience, but it was worth it the moment he saw Rudi's eyebrows raise.

'Do you really jump out of planes?'

'Yep.'

'No waaayyy.'

'Yeah, they don't like your car keys to fall out and end up hitting anyone.'

Rudi laughed. 'You're being daft. Is that really what you do?'

'Yes, honestly. I'm a tandem skydiving instructor – when I'm not hanging out and working on my découpage skills.'

'I can't imagine jumping out of a plane. It would be *so* cool!' Rudi's eyes were bulging. 'I'd love to do that. It would be awesome.'

'You would?'

'Yeah, but I never could.' Rudi glanced down at his découpage box, a flush of embarrassment reaching his cheeks.

'Why not?' Nathan's curiosity overtook the need to be polite.

The kid shrugged. 'Money and stuff. I need to be about for my dad.'

Rudi's response surprised Nathan. What a weight of responsibility for a young kid to bear.

'I'm afraid you have to be sixteen to jump, but there's always indoor skydiving in the meantime. In fact, you, Rudi, are my lightning bolt.'

'Your what?'

'I needed an idea and I think you've helped me find it.'

'What's that then?' Rudi was looking more than a little perplexed and had dipped his piece of paper in the glue for far too long.

'I'm going to have to look into it, but as far as I know, there are lots of jumps that take place in order to raise money for different charities, but I'm not sure if there are any charities that help people who need additional support to jump. You're a bit young currently, but it might be able to help you in the future.'

'I don't understand.'

'I'm not sure I do yet either. But I know what I need to do.' Nathan made sure Emma was paying attention when he said it. 'I'm going to set up a charity.'

In the past two days he'd met two people who would love to jump, but would never be able to without help of some kind. It was something he'd spent his life doing, and as far as he was concerned, it was the most freeing sensation in the world. The wind in his hair, the butterflies in his stomach, the world whizzing past – it was a gift, and one he wanted to share. He had to see what he could do to make it a possibility, and if he were clever, he might help far more than just those two people.

Chapter Fourteen

Day Ten

There was a baby crying.

Nathan woke with a start. Normally his dreams were strangely comforting in their familiarity, but this new noise at the end sent his pulse rushing.

The sound of crying filled his thoughts, even now he was awake. It had sparked an adrenaline rush he wasn't expecting, as if an intruder had entered his room without invitation. What had caused the noise?

Not quite able to get his bearings, Nathan opened his bedroom window. The hit of fresh air went some way to waking him up. Glancing along the suburban street, he tried to locate where the sound might have come from.

There was a park further along the road, and he often saw mothers bustling along the road with their buggies, toddlers in tow. Someone must have passed by, although all he was faced with now was a resounding silence. Only the tweeting of birds and the rustle of leaves filtered through.

Despite the stillness of the late morning, Nathan wasn't able to shift his feeling of unease. What if that sound hadn't been external? What if it was part of the dream? What did it mean if it was? If there was one thing the dream didn't do, it was change.

Nathan didn't want to dwell on it, especially given how unsettled it was making him feel. There were only a few aspects of his life that were consistent. His dream, however weird, was one of them. This shift meant he didn't know what to do with himself.

The only thing he could do was believe it was a mistake. Whatever he thought he'd dreamed, he hadn't, and he needed to distract himself.

But even the coldest blast of water from the shower wasn't enough to quieten his thoughts. He was stuck in a lost zone. Whereas he'd normally be getting ready for work, he was currently signed off following his recent panic attack. He'd not actually told his boss the truth about what had been the problem. When he'd phoned to check how he was, Nathan had spouted something about the hospital doctor signing him off because of low blood pressure. He wasn't sure why he'd said that when his sick note would say different. It was most likely because he wanted to get a green light on returning to work.

It was standard practice at his workplace that he would be subject to a medical when he returned, and it would no doubt come to light that what he'd said wasn't true. But somehow, when his boss had asked, a fixable problem seemed a preferable excuse to give. If there were consequences to not telling the whole truth, he'd have to deal with that when it came out. There was every chance he wouldn't be allowed to jump again.

With a towel wrapped around his waist, it was easy to peer at the small lump that was causing him to worry. In a few short days it would be gone. The procedure had been explained to him in depth. It was going to be done under a general anaesthetic, so that if they needed to take away any more tissue, they would be able to at the same time. He'd be left with a small wound which once healed would barely be noticeable.

Nathan got dressed quickly so he wasn't faced with the lump any more. He needed to channel his energies into more positive things. He needed to start looking into the possibilities of his idea. His everlasting act. At least that would be a distraction of sorts.

The drive to the skydiving centre was a welcome contrast to being stuck indoors. It was a cold day, but the skies were clear blue without a cloud in sight. There would definitely be a flight today. If he went now, he should time it just about perfectly not to bump into anyone – it wasn't hard to work out. He'd be able to speak to the people he wanted to without getting himself in trouble.

Knowing the charter was out made his task easy. There was only going to be one person in the building. There might be some guests, ready to watch their relatives hurl themselves out of a plane, but they would be outside at the viewing point, away from the main building.

It was something he shouldn't even be doing, and it might be an impossibility, but he had to scope it out to find out what the chances were. His charity idea was going to take a bit longer, but he wanted to see if he was able to organise something for Emma's mother in the meantime.

'Leanne, how are you?' It was good to see a friendly face and fortunately he knew Leanne would help him.

'OMG, Nathan, I've been sooo worried about you. Why haven't you replied to my messages?'

'I've not really messaged anyone, Leanne. I haven't really felt up to it.'

'Sorry to hear that. But does this mean you're better? Are you back?'

'Not exactly. I was hoping to see you, as I wanted to enlist your help. Any chance you can get this week's schedule up for me?' Nathan knew that attempting to pull off this jump would mean asking a lot of favours from his friends.

'But I thought you were signed off? You're not on any of the rotas at the moment.' Leanne went to her computer, happy to carry out the task despite her questions.

'No, I'm not due in to work yet. It's just…' Nathan wavered, unsure whether to say anything.

'What?' Leanne had noticed the hesitation and, in it, the opportunity to conspire.

Nathan took the risk. 'I'm hoping to keep it quiet – I'd rather Derek didn't know in case he wants me back to work before I'm ready – but I'm hoping to organise something for a friend. It might need to be on the down-low.'

He was afraid that, if Derek caught wind of him doing jumps, he would have something to say about him still being off work, even if this was a one-off.

Leanne opened up the work rota and pressed print. 'Why the secrecy? Although any secret of yours is safe with me.'

'Are there any days Derek is out this week? If I end up doing this jump, I just don't want him to know.' Their boss tended to work in chunks. Living further away than anyone else, he tended to cluster his days and stay nearby, and then he went back to his family in a four-on, four-off style system. It wasn't a work pattern he offered anyone else, but for once it might play to Nathan's advantage.

'He heads back home today,' Leanne said.

'That's great. Is that copy for me?' Nathan gestured towards the printer as it whirred away.

'Of course. And if there's anything Tim or I can do to help, you just let us know.' Leanne passed him the pieces of paper.

One rota secured. That was all he'd planned on achieving today. 'I have a feeling I'll be taking you up on that offer more than you can imagine.'

Leanne raised an eyebrow. 'Any chance you'll give me any clues about what you're planning?'

'I really want to help someone do a skydive, but it's an interesting set of circumstances. All I know is it feels like the right thing to do. A good deed, if you like.' Rightly or wrongly, he'd promised Emma's mother that he'd take her skydiving and he was determined to deliver on that promise, even if it did mean bending the rules.

The problem was that time wasn't on his side. Nor were medical notes. In this case he'd need to be medically certified as fit to work and Carole would need to be certified as fit to fly. They didn't have the luxury of waiting for either. If it was going to happen, it needed to be sooner rather than later. He'd do it by the rule book if he thought that was an option. But the awful sense of life closing in on him was getting stronger. If anything went wrong with his surgery, he might not be in a position to take Carole for a dive. And with the hoops they would have to jump through for someone with her condition, the delay might see it never taking place. It would be a good deed with a rebellious streak down the middle.

'We're all for good deeds. It brings good karma,' Leanne said.

The pilot and instructors were all his friends, and he knew that if he spoke with the rest of them, somehow they would pull it off. There was every chance he may not be able to dive again, so it made little difference to him if he got into trouble, but he didn't want to risk his friend's jobs. If they did it, they'd have to make sure they weren't caught.

'I think I'm definitely due some good karma,' Nathan said, but he didn't elaborate. He was keeping his cards close to his chest. No one ever wanted to admit they'd been dealt a hand as bad as the one that he thought he was holding. He was going to carry on bluffing for as long as he could.

Nathan's Diary

The problem has always been that my dream never changes. It's the same room. The same feeling. The same knowledge that today will be the day I take my final breath.

The repetition of the details brings it into focus – shining a beacon on the facts. There are no light-hearted dreams in-between to shift the pattern of this landscape.

There is the odd variation, some dreams choosing to reveal more nuances than others: a book on the bedside table, a picture on the wall, a person calling for help. Then there are the consistent elements, always there: the hospital room, the oxygen mask and the sensation of life leaving my body. These are the things that never change. These are the parts I rely on. The familiarities that have made me believe this is the truth. That I have no alternative in life. I have lived all my years knowing that this one will be my last. How can it not be, when I have never dreamed of a normal life... of camping or swimming or falling in love?

I've asked friends, I've Googled, I've even asked Alexa. They have all said the same thing: that while recurring dreams are not uncommon, having the same one all of your life isn't the norm. I'm yet to find a support forum for people with the same predicament.

That one dream.

On repeat.

The air leaving my lungs for the last time, almost every night.

So how can one variation make it a totally different dream? One detail, changing it entirely?

Hospital room.

Struggling to breathe.

A baby crying…

Chapter Fifteen

Day Fourteen

Emma

When Emma didn't hear from Nathan for a whole day, she tried to pretend like she wasn't at all worried.

Only she was.

It was strange how someone she had known for such a short length of time had become such a fundamental part of her existence. She'd shared more with Nathan than she had with anyone else. They might not have known each other long, but they'd already navigated more than some would do in an entire lifetime.

She had to remind herself that it had barely been two weeks since they'd met. It was perfectly normal not to hear from him all the time. They'd not known each other long enough for this to be significant. They weren't in a relationship; they were just friends. It wouldn't make any difference if he were to walk out of her life as quickly as he'd wandered into it.

Only it did matter. It *had* to matter.

Emma was walking to the corner shop in a futile attempt to stop herself from worrying about Nathan and whether he was okay. And of course, that took her nearer to his house, where they'd picked up the barbeque... Would it be too much to turn up there and hope he was in? At least it would put her mind at rest over hospital admissions.

It was silly how twenty-four little hours could seem so long. Yesterday she'd told her mum she'd taken the rest of the week off work to use up some annual leave. She'd ended up spending the day reading a book and checking her phone far too frequently. Now it was dinner time and she was far less organised than normal, as if all the rhythms of life had been knocked out of place.

Even though Emma was supposed to be picking some bits up for tea, the pull of wanting to know that Nathan was okay made her wander down his road. Out of habit as much as hope, she checked her phone again. No new notifications. She let out a sigh so loud a few birds flew out of a nearby tree.

The problem was that her concerns were genuine. The set of circumstances in which they'd met made anything out of the ordinary worrying.

Emma stared at Nathan's house for a while, deliberating whether knocking on his door was the best idea. She wasn't sure what she'd say if one of his housemates answered. But at least they might give her some idea of where he was.

From her pocket, Emma's phone chirped and she almost collapsed from the joy of receiving communication. Knowing her luck it would be a weekly marketing text to try and entice her into buying pizza.

Emma's anxieties physically eased as she read the message from Nathan, her shoulders lowering several centimetres. *Where are you?*

I'm at yours. Sorry, I should have called first, Emma replied.

Hah, I'm at yours! I want to talk to you.

Emma didn't hesitate in responding: *Coming!*

She scooted along the five-minute walk and managed it in three, wondering why he'd arrived unannounced and why he'd been off the radar.

When she arrived on Timberley Drive, it was easy to pick out Nathan's figure pressed against the garden wall of her house. As soon as he saw her, he headed in her direction.

She wanted to make a run for him. It was pretty sad, but seeing as he was real and not ignoring her like she'd thought he might have been, she longed to carry out an unadulterated display of affection. Something stopped her though. Probably the knowledge that such an act wouldn't be reciprocated. This was no scene from *Dirty Dancing*, even if she wanted it to be.

Nathan was bouncing when he reached her, like he'd drunk far too many coffees and all the caffeine molecules were trying to escape at once.

'Are you okay?' she asked.

'Yes, more than okay. I think I've worked it all out.'

'What exactly?' If it was the meaning of life, Emma wanted to know.

'I worked out what I want to do to raise money, or at least what I want to raise money for.'

'That's great. So what is it?' Emma wasn't sure what to do. It was the kind of occasion where she should invite him in, but as the front room doubled as her mother's bedroom, she didn't have anywhere to take him for a chat other than her bedroom, and she'd never got round to inviting a man into her private space. Living with her mum meant she'd never let anyone get this close. She wasn't about to either, so hanging round awkwardly on the pavement was going to have to suffice.

'I want to make sure that anyone who wants to go skydiving can do so without hurdles getting in the way. Whether that be physical, social or financial. I want to help lessen the barriers for anyone wanting to have a go.'

'That sounds amazing. I'm sure there are lots of people that would love to be given the opportunity. Do you know how you're going to raise money for that?' Emma had to admire his passion.

'That's what I've been doing today. I've been looking into how you go about setting up a charity and raising funds.'

'Is it a possibility?'

'It should be. And I'm hopeful your mum will be able to jump sooner. Do you think she'll be able to do it tomorrow evening?'

'That soon?' Perspiration formed on Emma's top lip at the thought. She wasn't keeping up with Nathan's eagerness. 'Why so quickly?'

Nathan placed a hand on Emma's shoulder. 'I'd really like to do the jump with her, and there's every chance that when my boss hears about my panic attack, he'll take me off the instructor team. I need to squeeze it in without him being aware of it. I only have two days before he's back and tomorrow's the only day I can trust everyone's discretion and get the help we'll need. I'm in for surgery before he goes away again and when he finds out about that I think he'll ground me for the time being.'

'Do you mean this isn't going to be entirely above board?'

'Not exactly.'

'Oh.' Emma was all for living life to the max, but she wasn't so sure it was a good thing for it to apply to her mother as well. 'Will she be safe?'

'I would never jump with her if I had any concerns. It will be safe for her to jump tandem with her condition. And as for me, that panic attack was a one-off thing, but if I have any issues I'll get one of my colleagues to take my place. I want to be the one to do this though. If this is going to be my last chance to jump, I want to do it as a gift to your mum.' Nathan peered at the house. 'And for you,' he added.

Emma didn't know what to say. There were so many things going through her head. She wasn't sure she liked the idea of it not being 'above board', or the thought of her mother hurtling through the air. But at the same time, if Nathan had been generous enough to organise it and it was something her mother wanted to do, who was she to stand in the way?

'What do you think then?' Nathan asked, obviously spotting the concern on Emma's face.

'It's not my decision to make. You need to talk to my mum and see if she's happy with this. She may have said she wanted to without realising you would really go ahead and organise something so quickly.'

'Shall we go and talk to her then? Is that okay?'

For all Emma's hesitation, she realised it wasn't her place to add limitations when life was doing so much of that already. If the opportunity was there, it was up to her mother whether she took it. 'We'll go and find out.'

'Great,' Nathan said, beaming. Emma wondered where she could purchase his level of enthusiasm.

'Mum, we have a visitor,' Emma called out as they both entered the house.

Whatever her mother's decision about skydiving at short notice, at least it was a distraction from the biggest hurdle that tomorrow had in store. Because even if Nathan and her mum were planning on throwing themselves out of an aeroplane, it wasn't going to be the scariest thing she would face.

The scariest thing would be the thing she'd been trying to distract herself from as much as possible. The thing that was coming whether she liked it or not. The thing that was no longer a thing, but an actual date and time that constituted an appointment.

Tomorrow, she would find out exactly how badly her world was about to unravel.

Nathan's Diary

Once was an anomaly. A freak occurrence. Something that could be blamed on other factors.

Twice is a pattern. Twice is an indicator that things have changed. Only I don't know how. And it scares me that I don't know what this dream means or what I should be doing about it.

Hospital room.

Struggling to breathe.

A baby crying…

Chapter Sixteen

Day Fifteen

Emma

Emma should have asked Nathan to come with her. It seemed a natural course of action to bring moral support along for such occasions. She was sure that, if she'd asked him, he would have said yes.

Now she was sitting in the waiting area, she was wondering why she hadn't. The reasons why seemed so lost and weak at this moment.

She hadn't asked because she'd decided this was her battle. He had his own challenges to face and she'd already dragged him into the worries of her world far too much. Why else would he be helping her mother jump out of a plane?

It was too late to ask him along now. And maybe facing it alone wasn't such a bad thing. There was bravery to be found in the solo act. And she would be able to live in denial a little longer if she was the only one who knew the reality.

Someone plonked their frame into the seat next to her.

'I thought you might need a copy of *Robot Wars Monthly*?'

Emma didn't hesitate in hugging Nathan. She didn't care what he or anyone else thought. Never had she been more pleased to see someone. The relief rippled through her and for a while she just let herself be held.

When she did pull herself together again, there was a little damp patch where her head had been resting.

Nathan placed the magazine in question on her lap.

Emma turned her attention to what he'd passed her. It didn't take much of an inspection for her to realise he'd mocked up his own version. 'What is this?'

The magazine was wrapped in a fabricated front and back cover like an old school textbook. But inside it was a copy of *Radio Times* with the listings for *Robot Wars* circled in neon pink highlighter.

'It's their trial edition. Personally, I think it needs some work.'

It was enough to make her want to turn into a puddle of emotions, but that would have to wait until later. He was a bright ray of hope in a waiting room that was void of such things.

If there was an option to wear warrior paint to oncology appointments, Emma would have slathered it on and given Nathan some for good measure. But for all the bravery she was trying to possess, there was nothing more fortifying than knowing she was going to have a hand to hold.

When her name was called, she was quite sure she floated up into a standing position. Because being brave didn't equate to this feeling real.

'Do you want me to come in with you?'

Emma nodded. She needed someone to keep her grounded as she drifted through the corridors and into the appointment room, where fate awaited her.

She took note of everything around her: the posters on the walls, the plastic skeleton in the corner keeping an eye on proceedings, the implements laid out on the table for checking reflexes and blood pressure alongside any other number of are-you-quite-alright instruments.

The scene was the same as in every other hospital appointment she'd ever been to. Apart from the fact that it was different. With every beat of her heart she was hearing new, unknown words. *Grade three. Radiotherapy. Surgery. Chemo.* Each piece of information made the pounding in her chest so loud she was barely able to take any of it in.

'In your case, we feel a unilateral mastectomy and reconstruction will be the best course of action in the first place, followed by a course of chemotherapy.'

Emma nodded, even though her head was numb.

'I know it's a lot to take in.'

She wasn't sure if she was taking anything in. Everything, including the doctor's appearance, was washing over her. She didn't want to take in the details of this moment. Even the facts were proving troublesome to keep hold of.

'As you may realise, the chemotherapy will come with some side effects, including loss of hair. There is also a chance it will affect your fertility, and as you and your partner are both young, that's something we need to discuss regarding what you'd like to do going forward.'

Emma and Nathan glanced at each other, but said nothing.

'Do you have any questions?'

Lost for words, Emma looked at Nathan to see if he was able to articulate better than she was.

'We probably need some time to process everything,' Nathan said, taking her hand in his.

'Of course. Like I said, it's a lot to consider. If at any point you have any questions or need to talk about anything we've discussed, our numbers are on the leaflets we've given you. Otherwise, we'll run through your questions and concerns at your next appointment. It might help if you write down anything you think of and bring your questions with you.'

There was a piece of paper in Emma's hand already. Not the magazine, but one of the leaflets they were talking about. She'd not even processed it making its way into her possession.

Emma only wanted them to fix her nipple, but whatever blind hope she'd had that it might just end up being some cosmetic surgery had flown out the window as soon as she'd walked in here and seen the cancer specialist nurse.

It was cancer.

War paint was going to be required.

Chapter Seventeen

Nathan

Smiling in the face of adversity, they called it. That was what Nathan liked to think he was doing. That whatever problem he had to face, he tackled it head on. He didn't like to think that life should be allowed to stand in the way. There were so often barriers to what people wanted to achieve and it was all too easy to give up at those hurdles.

Emma's diagnosis was just a hurdle.

They'd known that it was likely to be cancer.

Somehow, that didn't make it any easier.

The fact that he cared so much about the result meant he also cared far more for Emma than he was letting on. He wasn't sure how those feelings had crept up on him. He was all for jumping into things, especially with his line of work, but not when it came to relationships. And here he was unexpectedly harbouring feelings for someone he'd not long met.

Since he still had concerns over his own lump to deal with, developing anything else just couldn't be on the agenda – it would get far too messy. Today was about making someone else's dream possible. It wasn't about being selfish.

At least he'd spent his life doing as he pleased – not caring what others thought of him. Perhaps that was the gift his dream had provided him with. It had always given him the mentality of never taking no for an answer, of always achieving what he set out to do and not taking shit from anyone. Or perhaps it was a result of not having any close family. There was no one about these days to tell him to take care of himself. All his life he'd been regarded as a reckless troublemaker, and he was more than happy not to put that reputation to rest just yet.

That's why he was glad he was doing this today. Emma was still in a state of shock and they both needed something to provide them with a distraction. And even though it was breaking far too many rules, he wasn't going to let any barriers stand in the way of making it happen. Today, come hell or high water, Emma's mum was going to jump out of a plane.

There were four members of staff involved with the late-night jump. That was already more people than Nathan would have liked to involve, but certain things weren't possible without the assistance of friends. He wasn't foolish enough to try and pilot a plane by himself.

It was dark already, the February nights still drawing in early. Thankfully it was a clear sky, and although cold, the evening presented perfect jumping conditions, with a bright silver moon waiting for them along with its canvas of glittering stars. Everyone would be here soon. He'd not wanted to leave Emma after the hospital appointment but she'd insisted, and he needed to be here early to make sure everything was ready.

Alberto, the pilot, and his fellow diving instructors, Tim and Antonio, would return shortly. They'd agreed to leave work as usual, grab a bite to eat, then head back to get ready. They would be joined by Leanne so they had someone on the ground as well.

As Nathan finished the first set of safety checks, Antonio and Tim burst through the entrance with Leanne in tow.

'Are you sure about this, guys?' Nathan was addressing Leanne as well. Now was the time to abort the plan if they were worried. He didn't want to get anyone in trouble and it was always going to be a possibility.

'The CCTV is off. I've ordered an additional fuel load. As long as we keep it amongst us, Derek will never know this has happened,' announced Leanne.

'We're cool,' Antonio said.

'No worries,' Tim added.

Nathan nodded firmly, confirming the fact they were all in it together – as if that one gesture of his head would make it all go swimmingly.

It was just then that Emma and her mother made their appearance. Everyone moved to assist with holding doors open.

'Welcome, young lady. Are you ready for the adventure of a lifetime?' Antonio said with his usual abundant charm.

'You must be talking to my daughter,' Emma's mother giggled.

'A daughter? No, no, for you are far too young to have a daughter.' Antonio took Carole's shaking hand and planted a kiss on her knuckles, employing his intense stare that made women go weak at the knees.

But Nathan was focused on Emma, her eyes wide and lost in this new space. He pulled her close, weaving his arm round her delicate waist. Antonio wasn't allowed to woo all the ladies.

There was a resistance within Emma at first – a nod to the fact this wasn't the time or the place given the current format of their world. But that was only there for a fraction of a moment before she yielded and gave in to the need to be held.

'Let's go and make coffee. We'll get everyone a drink before we get started.' He swept Emma towards the staff room, realising she needed to be away from her mother if his hug was about to set her off crying.

'It's going to be okay,' Nathan said, repeating words that were so often lost in a landscape of uncertainty. 'We're going to get through this together.' He lifted her chin, as much for himself as for Emma. She didn't need to be alone. He was going to be here for her. 'Have you told your mum?'

There would never be a good time to tell her, but Nathan figured just before she was to jump out of a plane definitely wasn't the moment.

'No. I want to get some things in place for her before I do.' Emma wiped her face against his sleeve, removing whatever trace of upset she'd displayed. 'I don't want to think about it right now. We need to concentrate on you and my mum being completely crazy.' She managed to raise a half-smile.

'If you're sure? We don't have to do this.'

'Of course I am. Today needs craziness to improve its forecast.' Emma stretched her smile enough for him to know she was okay. Whatever news they'd been dealt today, they were going to deal with it in their own way.

She was the one smiling in the face of adversity.

Upon seeing her smudge of a smile, Nathan pulled her close. He felt more for her than he'd ever known was possible. It was hard to know she was hurting.

In reality, Nathan knew today hadn't really been about fulfilling Carole's desire to jump out of a plane. It had all been about keeping busy. This hadn't been about him trying to prove how selfless he could be despite a history that said otherwise. This wasn't about trying to get Carole on his side by proving anything was possible. This was about giving the woman he was falling in love with a reason to believe everything truly would be okay. That however impossible the road ahead seemed, they would find a way to conquer.

Everything would be okay.

Everything had to be okay.

Chapter Eighteen

Everything was okay.

It was just the stakes were higher with this jump. And as this would probably be his last, Nathan didn't want anything going wrong. If it did, they were bound to get in trouble, and there were risks to people's jobs as well as all the usual ones associated with chucking bodies out of a plane at 120 miles per hour.

Those concerns went as soon as they leapt. Then there weren't even thoughts, only the glorious sensation of falling.

The gush of wind.

The friction of limbs fighting the forces.

The adrenaline pumping through his veins.

The flip of his stomach as he tried to stay in control.

The tension in his arm as he pulled the pilot chute to stabilise their decent.

The whoosh enough to lose every sense for a second.

But this time, the magic wasn't in what he'd experienced hundreds of times before... It was in the poise of Emma's mum.

Because rather than any of the problems he'd been concerned she might experience, the usual myoclonic movement of her muscles unfurled, as if she were a swan out on a May Day parade. She truly was a bird in flight.

It was grace itself. It was freedom. It was like nothing he'd ever witnessed before.

Jumping was a gift Nathan had never fully appreciated. He'd always wanted to do daredevil things. Now that freedom was coming to an end, it was as if all his skydives were merging into this one final, poignant, plummeting-through-the-sky memory.

As he took in the great canvas of glimmering stars against the inky black sky, it was enough to make him want to cry. If his time was limited, he was going to make sure he did two things while still on the planet.

First, he would make sure Emma got to do her everlasting act. If she wanted to see puffins, he would make it happen.

Second, he would make sure, even if he didn't, that Emma would survive this. Because at least one of them had to.

Chapter Nineteen

Emma

Fed up with remaining inside the viewing area, Emma ventured out the doors to find a spot to wait. Leanne had said it would be fine for her to go out, but she needed to remain at the desk, her safety checks keeping her there.

It was good to be outside. A fresh whip of air caught Emma in the face and reminded her she was alive. Perhaps it was because she spent so much time inside these days that she valued being out and exposed to the elements. The wind was blowing at a temperature that made her feel like icy liquid was being poured on her cheeks, the coolness dissipating as soon as it arrived. Boy, did she need it at this moment in time.

Then she heard it. Faint at first, gradually becoming more pronounced...

'Whhhhhhhheeeeeeeeeeeeeeeeeeeeeeeeeeeeeeeeeeeeeeeeeeeeeee!'

It was coming from the sky above her, and it was unmistakably her mother making her way back to the earth.

Letting her eyes follow the noise, it wasn't long before Emma made out the figures flying through the air.

Emma had been filling her head with bad outcomes: her mum being sick mid-air or breaking a limb on landing or Nathan having another panic attack. But as she watched their descent, she soon realised the opposite was true. In the glare of the floodlights, they appeared like a powerful eagle swooping into a stadium, ready to win. There would be no stopping them, and the sound of joy her mum was emitting echoed all around her. She wanted to record it and keep it forever. What a moment. What a moment to cherish and fold up in a pocket and hold on to for all time.

As they whooshed ever closer to the ground, Emma was filled with a warm flush of relief.

Nathan was elegantly manoeuvring her mother into a landing with ease, her small frame curled up like a child's and his limbs long enough to carry it out without her help. Their landing was more like unicorns cantering on soft fluffy pillows than any of the hundred awful scenarios Emma had imagined.

Listening to her mother's continued exclamations of joy, Emma realised she wanted that. Not to jump out of a plane – she wasn't about to turn that insane any time soon, cancer or not – but she wanted to have that feeling. That unreserved joy. That freedom.

With that thought, Emma joined the two most important people in her life, lying next to them so they were all looking up at the stars. She positioned herself parallel to them and slipped her hand into her mother's, Nathan placing his strong, solid hand on Emma's shoulder. Even though she hadn't hurtled herself through the air, in that moment she felt their adrenaline coursing through them. It was settling now they were on the ground. And as that rush came down all around them, Emma was able to make out Orion in the sky. The constellation was twinkling brighter than it ever had before, as if the energy they had produced in their skydive was charging it with added intensity. As if somehow their jump had brought the stars that much closer. As if the miracle of what had occurred had been noted by the stars themselves.

'That was amazing. You two were really awesome.'

Emma's life definitely needed more awesome, but right at that moment, she needed to appreciate all the awesome that existed in her loved ones. The rest of life's nonsense deserved to be ignored. At least for the moment. Because right now they were busy absorbing the magic of a night sky all of their very own.

Nathan's Diary

Is it weird that I'm glad it was the last jump? I thought I'd be distraught that I might never get the chance to do it again. That somehow it would be like severing a limb... Instead, there is relief.

I no longer have to be the adrenaline junkie, fuelled by the ecstasy of others. The need to chase the coat-tails of the extreme has left me. And I'm glad. Because sometimes something ending isn't a bad thing. Sometimes it represents a change for the better.

I wish the dream would resolve as succinctly. It's hard to see straight when something has been pressing on your thoughts for so long. If I went a week without it keeping me company at night, perhaps I'd see how ludicrous it is to believe what my imagination is pumping out.

I wish it would end and provide me with a new beginning.

Instead, I'm forever reminded about my own mortality. Of how this is the year it all ends.

And what am I supposed to make of this change? Of the baby's cries in my dream? Because I can't help but feel it all has to be for a reason. Otherwise why would I keep dying every time I dream? Why would that baby be crying other than to pinch at my conscience to the point it is screaming?

Today it's time for the lump to go. And I can't help but feel that dread. Because perhaps it is also the day the dream comes to fruition...

Chapter Twenty

Day Twenty

Nathan

'There have to be better transport options than this,' Nathan said. Today they were going for the double. Emma had her follow-up and Nathan had his surgery.

Nathan's stomach was grumbling. He wasn't allowed to eat prior to surgery, but he already knew he was last on the list, as they'd been kind enough to schedule things so that he was able to join Emma for her appointment.

There were proving to be many advantages to the medical staff believing they were a couple.

'We're on here now. Stop moaning. Anyway, it's good for the environment.'

Nathan didn't want her to think he was some kind of transport snob, but there was a distinct smell of urine and he was unable to work out if it was coming from the upholstery or a guy a few rows down.

It was making him wonder if there had been any point to the shower he'd had this morning with some kind of antibacterial solution the hospital had given him. Clearly he was coating himself with all sorts of germs on this choice of transport. Driving wasn't an option as he wouldn't be allowed to on their return and Emma didn't feel confident about driving a car as old as his. As he hadn't told a single other soul yet, they were opting not to call on anyone's help. And even though Emma had her results, she'd wanted to arrange some extra care for her mother prior to telling her, so there would be one less thing for Carole to worry about.

'Promise me we can get a taxi on the way back. No open wound is going to survive this environment.'

'I don't think it's classed as open when it's stitched up and covered with a dressing.'

'Even so, I think it will aid my recovery if I don't have to face this on my return.'

'It stinks, doesn't it?'

'It really does.'

Joking about the stench of urine made Nathan smile. He hadn't thought that would be possible today. He was disproportionately concerned about the straightforward procedure he was due to have. It wasn't major surgery. It wasn't even in the same ballpark as the mastectomy they were talking Emma through today. But there was that black cloud that followed him everywhere these days... This was the year in which he died.

'I don't have to be there for another forty-five minutes. Let's get off now. We've got enough time to walk the rest of the way,' Emma said.

Her words broke Nathan from his melancholy. They'd got the earlier bus so as not to be late. He wasn't sure why either of them was in such a hurry to get to appointments they'd rather not face. 'I've never wanted to make a break for freedom more.'

When they tumbled off the bus together they both took the biggest breath of fresh air.

'I'm pretty sure I haven't taken a proper lungful of air since we got on that bus. You're lucky I didn't pass out on you.' Nathan wasn't even joking. Considering his recent experience with panic attacks, he really should be trying to avoid not breathing properly.

'Same here. There aren't many smells so bad that not taking oxygen on board seems like a good option.' Emma's frame was slender, like a ballerina. She'd be light as a feather to catch, but it wouldn't help if he passed out alongside her.

After a few more breaths, they headed off up the hill towards the hospital. Although getting sweaty was also undoing the good of his morning shower, it was still one hundred per cent preferable to remaining on the bus with all the urine particles that might have been landing on his skin.

It wasn't a steep hill, so it wasn't really a workout. But everything seemed to take much more effort of late. As if that one small lump was weighing him down and making even the simplest tasks difficult.

Despite how he was feeling, there were still signs everywhere that spring was beginning to awaken. The branches of cherry blossom trees were filling with pink buds as another year of seasons was set to start its cycle.

Nathan slipped his hand into Emma's. He didn't think about it, and yet as he did it he knew it was the right thing to do. They were in this together. If she didn't know that by now, he wanted to make sure she did. 'How are you feeling?'

'I should be asking you that, shouldn't I?'

'I think we both get to ask the question.' Nathan recognised that she was avoiding answering. And he couldn't blame her. '*How are you feeling?*' was such a naff way to open up conversation given what they were faced with.

'It doesn't feel real. My brain doesn't seem to think any of this is plausible. I'm about to go into an appointment to discuss having my boob removed. It's not even remotely close to the kind of thing I should be enjoying at this point in life.'

'That reminds me. We need to check that it's okay for us to go off on a jaunt beforehand.'

'What are you on about?'

'Your everlasting act… You said you wanted to go and see puffins. I'm going to make sure that we do.'

'But you need to concentrate on today even more than me. Stop avoiding the question – how are you feeling?'

'I think we might both be guilty of that. Well, as we know, my day involves having my third nipple removed. The less I think about that the better.' Although he hadn't lived with it for long, he was going to be glad to have it gone, even if the thought of being a patient in a hospital room terrified him.

'Are you sure you want to come to my appointment? I doubt hearing about my situation is going to provide much of a distraction.'

They were coming up to the bridge of the hill. There was only a corner to turn and then the great hulk of the hospital would be in view.

Nathan stopped, not quite ready to turn the corner just yet. He didn't know what to do with himself. He wanted to hold her. He wanted to kiss her. He was normally a natural when life called for such things, but instead he was staring at her like a moron. 'I'm going to be there for you. The same as you're there for me.'

'Thank you. And thank you for what you did for my mum. It truly was the most amazing thing.' Emma glanced down at their intertwined hands, as if she sensed Nathan's awkwardness. 'I can still hear her squeals of delight. Everyone deserves a moment like that.'

Nathan looked Emma directly in the eyes and placed his hands on her shoulders. 'You'll get your moment. And we'll make sure lots of other people will as well. We just need to get today out of the way first. We just need to tackle one step at a time.'

If he thought about everything they were facing, it would soon get overwhelming. One step at a time seemed like good advice, but he was all too aware they were leaning over a chasm.

With his hands on Emma's shoulders, Nathan was in no rush to move. The expression on Emma's porcelain face was the most important thing in the world. Tendrils of hair blew against her pale cheeks.

He brought his lips down to meet hers, not quite reaching that last quarter, leaving a gap for her to bridge. He wasn't going to force a kiss on her – that should never happen – even though every particle of him wanted their lips to meet. It would be a reminder of what it was to be alive – a reminder he longed for right now.

Emma eased herself fractionally closer. Not so much that the kiss was complete. Just enough for Nathan to realise that maybe he wasn't the only one who felt there was something pulling them together.

And just as that thought made his heart flutter, Emma pulled away. 'We can't. We shouldn't.'

'Why not?' Nathan's disappointment carried through to his response. He was always in favour of listening to his instincts, even if it had been known to get him into trouble. Right now, he was very much in favour of getting into trouble.

'You've sanitised, for starters. You don't need me adding to your germ load pre-surgery. And plus, we don't need to add to our worries. We've both got procedures to get through. We don't need the added pressure of a relationship starting between us.'

'You're right. This isn't the time or the place to start something. It was just a moment. Spontaneity took over me.' But with every word, Nathan was moving closer to her, not further away. Or was she getting closer after all?

'It's not the time or place at all,' Emma whispered, as their lips met for the first time.

It didn't take any thought to embrace the softness of Emma's kiss, the gentle yet intense pressure making every part of him feel alive. The slow sweep of her tongue; the taste of spearmint. But there were thoughts seeping through. Because this wasn't just any kiss… It was a perfect one. It was telling him a story… It was telling him that somehow this act was going to merge them together, and somehow they would be able to save one another.

If only he knew how.

Chapter Twenty-One

Emma

Kissing Nathan was the first time Emma really understood the concept of her heart ruling her head. It was also the first time she'd known what it was to be properly kissed.

Emma hadn't been able to resist, but she wasn't able to ignore the thoughts running through her head, telling her the timing wasn't right. Not when they both needed to be concentrating on their health first and foremost. And yet when his lips reached hers, there had been nothing she'd wanted more. And given what she was facing, she knew she had to learn to live a little.

Once they'd unlocked lips, they'd wandered the rest of the way to the hospital hand-in-hand, her fingers tingling. It didn't seem real now they were sitting waiting for Emma's appointment. But it was going to be easier to face it while holding Nathan's hand, with the taste of his kiss still on her lips.

Emma and Nathan had barely been on their seats long enough for the padded cushions to mould into the shapes of their butts before someone called for Emma to come in.

It was the same nurse who'd been in the room on diagnosis day.

'What was your name again?' Emma asked, deciding she needed to be a bit more awake to facts and details this time. She wasn't going to be able to live in denial forever.

'I'm Miranda, your specialist nurse. I work alongside Dr Howson. Please take a seat.'

The room was the same one as before. The same information posters on the wall; the same instruments on the doctor's desk. Emma had been hoping for something a bit cosier. Something more like home. Hopefully that came further along in the we-need-to-lop-your-boob-off journey.

Trying to think about it in a tongue-in-cheek kind of manner was the only way she was coping with this. Because the reality was too much to bear. She would bear it, of course she would – she would do whatever was within her power to do. But it didn't seem fathomable that this was a battle she was facing in her twenties, and when her mother needed her the most.

'Hopefully you've had a chance to read the information leaflets we gave you?' Dr Howson asked. Emma shook her head. 'I've been helping my mum skydive,' she said, as way of explanation. It was an excuse really. She'd not wanted to look through any of the facts she'd been offered. She hadn't been able to face up to any of it.

'Okay. If you could manage to before your next appointment, you might find it helpful. They give a good explanation as to what to expect. As discussed before, we plan to go for a mastectomy. We've discussed your case and my colleagues have agreed that surgery and chemotherapy will be the most appropriate course of action.'

Nathan squeezed Emma's hand. It was the reassurance she needed while she was trying not to smart at being referred to as a 'case'.

'The good news is the tests are back and we're not looking at a hormone-related cancer. That means we can go ahead and investigate the possibility of protecting your future fertility. We'll refer you to Wessex Fertility Clinic if that is something you want to explore prior to starting your chemotherapy. It means we'll be able to freeze some of your eggs for the future. We can refer your partner as well, as if we put your samples together, frozen embryos tend to have a better chance of a positive outcome than the eggs alone.'

The information was hurtling towards Emma too fast and too strong and too scarily. She'd barely even managed to process the fact that because of one dodgy nipple they were going to remove her breast. Now he was asking about a future she'd never even considered – having children. With Nathan. A man she barely knew.

'I'll let you talk this through further with Miranda. We'll get a date for surgery arranged as soon as possible and start to get things underway. Lovely to see you both again.'

The doctor extended his hand out for Emma to shake, but all she was able to do was stare at it and try not to think about them being the hands that would be operating on her. No, there was a better way to look at it. They were the hands that would save her from cancer. The hands that would save her life.

She shook the doctor's hand, repeating the reassurance in her head: *These are the hands that will save me from cancer. These are the hands that will save my life.*

She had to believe that. There was no room to think anything else.

'I'm sorry Dr Howson had to rush off.' Miranda the nurse took the place of the doctor, a more comforting presence with her friendly smile and rosy cheeks. 'Can I get you both a drink? A cup of tea to give you some time to mull over any questions you want to ask me?'

'Yes, please,' Nathan said.

Emma was still staring at her fingers.

'Are you okay?' asked Nathan, once they were alone.

'I just…' She didn't have words. 'A mastectomy.'

'It must be a lot to get your head round.'

Emma looked down at the curve of her chest. She'd never felt her breasts defined her womanhood, but she wasn't sure how she would feel without one. Her flat nipple already left her incomplete: a jigsaw without all the pieces in place. 'I just don't know how I'm going to feel.'

'The nurse will talk to you about the next stage and how they'll go about reconstruction.'

'You're more in the know than me.' Emma didn't want to sound so self-pityingly miserable, but right now she couldn't muster anything else.

'I knew you wouldn't want to, so I read through those leaflets. I figured one of us should have some idea what was going on.'

At least someone was looking after her. She should have been brave enough to look after herself, but sometimes life left all resources out of reach. She didn't have the capacity to take it all in without help.

Miranda entered the room, bringing mugs of tea with her. 'How are you both getting on? I thought I'd give you time to drink your tea, and then if you have questions or concerns we can go through them.'

There was no part of Emma's life that she wasn't concerned about. If she wrote it all down she would cry a river and still have enough salty tears left over to fill another mug.

'Thanks,' Nathan said, since Emma was only blinking, unable to utter a word. Miranda left again, and it was just them.

They were silent for a while.

They were back to where they'd started: two people who'd met in a waiting room.

Two people with lumps that shouldn't be there. Nathan's would be removed this afternoon. Maybe, with it, their connection would be gone. They would go back to being strangers.

'Why do they think we're partners? We could be siblings, for all they know,' Emma asked, thinking of their first kiss just an hour ago, the taste of his lips still lingering on hers.

'Because we haven't said otherwise?'

'But we haven't said we are.' Emma couldn't stop thinking about the fertility treatment. About what it meant. About why it was necessary. About what ten years from now might look like, if it even existed.

Nathan scratched his knee before turning his gaze to Emma. 'I've put you down as my partner on my next of kin. That might be why.'

'Oh.'

'I did it when I got admitted to A&E. For the panic attack. I didn't want anyone else knowing, and because you were picking me up and because I don't really have any other close family members…'

'It's okay.'

'Are you mad at me? I'm sorry. It just seemed logical at the time.'

'It's okay.'

'And we kind of are. Partners, that is. In this, if nothing else.'

Emma had never had a partner. She'd never come close. 'Do you think we'll make it through this?'

It was too big a question. It was too unquantifiable. How did anyone ever know where life was going to take them when it wasn't always possible to be in the driving seat?

'One day at a time. Hell, let's break it down to one hour at a time. That's all we can do.'

'And that's why we should never waste an hour?'

'Never. Which is why we should say yes to the fertility referral.'

Emma had been so busy coping with her mother that she'd never thought about having kids herself. Dates had never developed into relationships, so it wasn't like she'd ever been in that position. Not even close. But in the face of everything that was going on, it seemed only right to grab hold of this one glimmer of light.

'Together?' Emma asked.

'Because we're partners.' Nathan raised his mug to hers and chinked them as if they'd just come to some business agreement.

'Partners,' Emma repeated, unsure of which variety they were, but accepting at that moment it didn't matter.

The only thing that mattered was that they kept fighting.

Chapter Twenty-Two

Nathan

Even though Nathan was all dressed up in a hospital gown with only a cannula for company, he wasn't able to think of anything other than Emma as they wheeled him to the theatre. Kissing her had been the right thing to do. It had been a perfect moment. One he wished to live over and over. But it wasn't powerful enough to push away the fear.

There was no escaping the fact he was drawing closer to the point he thought was inevitable. This was his last year. It was only a matter a time before he would draw his last breath.

He just had to hope it wasn't too soon. Or too late to tell Emma about his concerns.

Hospital room.
Struggling to breathe.
A baby crying...

Chapter Twenty-Three

Emma

Writing a list with a pen and paper couldn't distract her, but Emma had to do something to occupy her mind while she waited for Nathan. She realised her fingers were crossed. She was holding onto the hope that once Nathan's lump was removed, that was all the treatment he would require.

Emma's surroundings weren't helping the time pass. The day surgery ward was a room with six beds and poor lighting. The cubicles were separated by flimsy curtains, and as each patient was seen, there wasn't much chance of not hearing what procedure they were having done. Nathan's bed was by the window, but the view was only of another brick building, so that wasn't providing any distraction. She would be so glad when they got out of here. After today, getting home had never been a more refreshing thought.

He should have been out by now. All being well, they'd said he would be back on the ward by two, but the clock had passed that point a quarter of an hour ago.

So to fill her time, she was writing down a to-do list for Nathan's charity idea. They'd been so occupied they'd not talked about it further. It was nice to have a practical thing to focus on to help distract her from the lump in her throat and the tears threatening to spill at any moment.

- Decide on a name
- Set up a charity number
- Open a charity bank account

Emma scratched out bullet points on the page and doodled trees and flowers round each one with far more detail than she would ever normally stretch to.

Generally, when she made plans, it was with the help of books. She'd been a bookworm since she was a kid and had spent countless hours daydreaming about future quests or gaining infinite knowledge on subjects she knew nothing about.

It had worked. She had spent entire days as a geisha and evenings at Lake Garda, and had kissed sexy vampires for a bit of variety. She'd reached more exotic corners of the world than she could name and a few worlds beyond the one in which she existed. But did any of that help her to leave a mark on life? Even her dream to see puffins seemed so small next to Nathan's desire to set up a charity. It wasn't about comparisons though. It was about doing something they both truly desired. And it was giving Emma something positive to think about.

Or at least she was trying to think about it. But something was throwing her off. That kiss. His lips. The talk of being partners. Had she inadvertently, on the worst day of her life thus far, ended up bagging herself a man? If that wasn't a silver lining, she didn't know what was.

The kiss. The softness of his lips on hers. That connection made complete. She didn't have much experience in such matters, but somehow she knew that kissing didn't get much better than that.

Giving up on trying to progress Nathan's plans, she started doodling again instead. As usual, she drew puffins. It was strange to have such an affinity with an animal she'd never seen. She put it down to its association with books from her childhood and the colour of its bill. Her mother had bought a Puffin series for her and she'd loved those books until they were worn out. Seeing the image so often, curled up in bed with it every night, meant she'd always wanted to see one in the wild. It seemed like such an odd creature to exist on the British Isles – she didn't even need to get on a plane to see one in its natural habitat. She just hadn't ever got round to doing it. Like so many other things in her life.

A patient was wheeled back into the day ward. Emma should be concentrating on writing helpful lists. Although that was easier said than done. Especially since Nathan still wasn't out of surgery.

The patient wasn't Nathan, and Emma started to get restless. Even though she didn't believe that Nathan's dream was an actual prediction of the future like he did, she still felt apprehensive. If Nathan truly believed it, couldn't it become a self-fulfilling prophecy? If that concept was so fixed in his head, if he thought nothing would make any difference to the eventual outcome, would he even want to have treatment?

As one hour became two, and then three, these worries whirred and buzzed around her head. Several times the nurse came along with reassurances that she'd let Emma know as soon as she heard anything.

Just as she was about to enquire again, the nurse walked over to where she was sitting. Rather than speak to her straight away, she made the effort to pull the curtains around. They scrapped against the metal with the horrid sound of nails scratching across a chalkboard.

Emma wasn't sure why; it wasn't like the flimsy material would stop everyone else in the unit from hearing what was about to be said. But it didn't seem like a good sign.

'I've just heard back from the doctors. They've decided to keep Nathan in. Once he comes out of recovery he'll be going to ward D4.'

Every hair on Emma's body rose in alert. It was a simple procedure. She shouldn't be hearing news like this today. 'What happened?'

The nurse looked like she didn't know what to say.

Chapter Twenty-Four

Nathan

Bright lights.

Searing pain.

A cut down Nathan's side.

A rib on display.

The slice of a scalpel.

A tube in his mouth.

This wasn't how the dream should go.

Nathan didn't like this new ending.

This new ending was panic and pain.

It wasn't gasping for breath; it was grappling at whatever was in his mouth to get it out. To make this stop.

Nathan was deep inside the matrix and his only way out was to fight and fight hard.

He pushed against the arms that held him. He attempted to shout above the voices that were booming instructions. He employed everything within him in order to survive, because however accepting he was of the idea of death, this was not how it was meant to happen. He was certain of that.

This wasn't a dream. This was a nightmare.

Chapter Twenty-Five

Emma

Nathan didn't look the same when he was unconscious. His skin was a shade paler. His hair a touch darker. His muscles slack.

Emma didn't want to leave him there. It seemed wrong to when he looked so helpless. If she'd had any idea that this was going to happen, she would have had the foresight to sort out someone to care for her mother.

She had his hand held between hers. Apart from its warmth, it was as lifeless as the rest of him. 'I need to go back and sort Mum out. I should be able to come back later. Hopefully you'll be more awake by then.'

She wasn't even sure if Nathan could hear her. If he understood that she had to go home for her mother.

He'd been heavily sedated after waking during his procedure. They'd expected him to be stirring already, but thus far the effects of the extra sedation hadn't worn off. It was heartbreaking to see the active, energetic, handsome man she knew reduced to this. She'd never even seen him sleeping before.

She lingered, not wanting to leave him, in the same way she didn't want to abandon her mother.

In the end, it was the logistics that secured her decision. Even though Nathan was asleep, at least he wasn't alone and fending for himself. The nursing staff were there to look after him, whereas her mother was alone. If anything were to happen to her, Emma would never forgive herself.

She treated herself to a taxi journey. Nathan would have been proud of her. It was getting late and she wasn't in a fit enough state to deal with other people or any of the plethora of variables the bus journey often presented.

And for the first time in a very long time she wanted her mum. She was so used to looking after her that she'd become quite independent. It tended to be her mother who needed her, not the other way round. But right now she'd do anything for a hug from her. More had been piled into her little universe today than she'd ever thought possible.

As soon as she got home she felt the tears come. She'd managed to bottle them up right until she crossed the threshold, and then they were unleashed in a great rush.

'Come here, baby.'

On hearing the upset, Carole had managed to do something she was barely capable of any more – she had wheeled herself towards the hallway.

'Oh, Mum. You'll end up hurting yourself.'

'Never mind that. Come here and tell me what's going on.'

Emma rested her head on her mother's lap and let her hair be stroked. Where did she even start? Because she realised that whatever she said about Nathan meant giving a full disclosure of everything that was going on. It was time her mum knew.

It wouldn't be an easy thing to do, but right at that moment Emma no longer knew what she was protecting her mother from. She'd thought of her as a fragile person who might not be able to withstand seeing her daughter going through such an ordeal. She'd had it in her head that, as well as possibly finishing her off, it might finish her mother off as well.

But her mother wasn't that person. She didn't need to be constantly coddled and cared for. She was much stronger than that. This was the woman who jumped out of planes for kicks. While her body might not be as capable as they'd like it to be, her mental strength was far beyond anything Emma had witnessed before.

'I'm really sorry, Mum. I should have told you before.' Emma was surprised to find that cohesive sentences escaped her lips. But then she stalled. How should she sum up everything that she needed to say?

'Whatever it is, you can tell me. What's happened with Nathan? Are you okay?'

Emma realised there was only one real place to start, and that was the beginning.

'Nathan and I didn't really meet on the bus.' The tale that followed seemed to be endless. She explained how they'd met, how Nathan had volunteered to be with her for her examination and how she'd repaid the favour. She explained that she'd had her results and the news wasn't good, that there would be surgery and treatment taking place in the weeks ahead. Though she'd struggled to find the words to start with, they soon found their way out in a barrage of information and tears.

'Oh, sweetheart. Why didn't you tell me before? What a thing to endure all by yourself.'

Emma was sobbing to the point her nose was dripping. 'But I've had Nathan. Until today.'

'What's happened to Nathan? Don't tell me…' Emma's mum looked horrified as the unimaginable, unutterable thought ran through her.

'No, not that. He had his procedure today to remove his lump. It was supposed to be day surgery and he should have been in and out. Only it wasn't as straightforward as they hoped it would be.'

'What happened?'

Even though they were in an uncomfortable position, with Carole's wheelchair in the lounge doorway and Emma curled into her lap with her bottom in the hallway, they didn't move. There was no point moving until the whole story was told.

'He woke up during the procedure. He was sedated to the required level for his build, but apparently it wasn't as effective as normal. He woke up thrashing and trying to pull the ventilator out of his mouth. They had to put him under heavy sedation to complete the operation and now he's not waking up.'

It sounded horrible out loud. Nathan had experienced what no person ever should. Emma couldn't even imagine the pain. She hoped that when he woke up he wouldn't remember.

'What are you doing back here? You should be with him.'

'I couldn't leave you by yourself. I needed to come back and sort you out.' Emma felt more useful here than she had there. She hadn't known what to do with herself in the hospital, faced with such an unexpected, horrifying set of circumstances.

'My girl, you have got to stop doing everything for me to the detriment of yourself.' Emma's mother paused for a moment, swallowing down emotions that were yet to surface. 'Is Nathan by himself? Does he have any family with him?' Although she hadn't known Nathan for long, much like Emma, she had a soft spot for him already.

'His mum died when he was born and his dad hasn't ever really been part of his life. He's only got a half-brother who he isn't really in contact with. He's got me down as his next of kin because he knew his brother wouldn't be interested in what was going on. They're not close at all.'

'We need to go to the hospital then. He can't be there by himself. If his family can't be about, then we'll be his family.'

'But we haven't pre-booked a car?' Whenever they headed to her mother's hospital appointments, it was always a planned outing – anything unplanned tended to be in the back of an ambulance with a screaming siren.

'The buses are still running. And it's late enough that the wheel-chair space won't be filled with buggies. We can eat in their canteen. Come on, sweetie. You can't be *here* when you need to be *there*.'

Even though her mother needed help with navigating the wheelchair along the road and onto the bus, for the first time in a long while she put herself in charge. She was being Mum, her maternal instinct to take control, to help her daughter, coming to the fore.

Emma hadn't realised it was what she'd needed. The idea of telling her mother about her cancer and the complexities it would cause them had been too overwhelming to face. She realised now it was because she'd already written her mum off.

It was wrong of her, she was aware of that now, but she'd defined her mother as incapable because of her disability. She'd thought that finding out her daughter was ill would perhaps make her condition worse. Perhaps that was still a possibility, but for now she was witnessing something else. As her mum instructed her every step of the way to the hospital, she was watching the fight-or-flight reflex in action. It turned out her mother would never be someone who ran away from life's problems. She was gloved up and ready to take action in whatever way she was able to.

Perhaps it required taking flight for the fight to kick in. When her mother had flown through the sky, there was no doubt she had been reunited with her spirit on the way down. Whatever zest for life had been lost along the way seemed to have returned, just at the point they all needed it.

When they returned to Nathan's bedside, there was no change. He was still pale. His hair was flat and unmoving. Everything without his usual characteristic bounce. He looked like he was sleeping and yet Emma knew he wasn't.

'Why isn't he awake yet?' Emma wasn't able to hide the despair in her voice. Surely people were supposed to wake up in the recovery room, and when they got to the ward they should be up and chatting and drinking tea and eating toast.

'The doctors think the sedation is taking a little longer to leave his body than usual. Rest assured he is being monitored closely.'

The nurse's words were no reassurance whatsoever.

'When do you expect him to wake up?' Emma's mother asked with a steady tone, something that her daughter was unable to muster.

'It could be anytime, but he needs to sleep it off and his system needs to get over the extra dose of sedative he's had. He should be back to normal by tomorrow morning.'

They both returned to Nathan's bedside none the wiser. Emma took hold of his hand and in turn her mum held her hand.

Somehow it was all a little easier with her mother by her side. In this fight-or-flight world, they were choosing to fight – together.

Nathan

I wish I was able to write down these words. I wish I could send them to you instead of them being trapped.

Right now, I am lost.

Not in the daily grind. Somewhere else. Somewhere not here.

And it isn't the dream — not the one I've been trapped in for the past twenty-seven years.

There is birdsong trying to bring me home. A gentle, persistent chirping. It won't let me rest here. It wants me to come back to you. It's calling me to the landing square. It promises that if I follow the path, lit up by the floodlights, it will welcome me with open arms.

But there are times when you are too lost to follow the birdsong. Too tired to find the right path. There are times when you're on the verge of giving up.

Chapter Twenty-Six

Day Twenty-Three

Emma

Emma had taken to reading to Nathan. It was now day three, and clearly whatever was happening to him wasn't usual after a routine surgical procedure.

The worst part was even the doctors seemed baffled. It made it very hard to gauge whether anyone should be concerned, and to what level. There were mostly mutterings about it being down to shock.

Because she wasn't, strictly speaking, next of kin, Emma had asked the nursing staff to get in touch with Nathan's half-brother, Marcus. But Nathan hadn't been kidding when he said his brother wouldn't be interested – Marcus was a royal idiot. When Emma had called him, he had said that unless Nathan was dying, he didn't see the point in visiting. He didn't even want to be updated. When Nathan had spoken about Marcus before, he'd told Emma that because their father had never played a part in Marcus's life, his half-brother had never wanted anything to do with the man's history either. Nathan had tried to play a supportive role by being the one to make contact and establish some kind of sibling relationship, but it had all been rebuffed. It seemed pretty dismal to Emma that, even given that Nathan was ill, Marcus wasn't prepared to forgive the mistakes of their father. It didn't seem right when neither of them was to blame.

Instead, Marcus had questioned Emma about who she was and why she was down as next of kin. It was sad that he didn't know much about Nathan's life. The problem was, neither did Emma. She knew the basics: where he worked, where he lived and a few of the people he would call friends. On day two of his sedation, she'd gone round to his place to speak to his housemates. She knew some of his friends at his workplace, but she thought it was best not to tell them yet, not without Nathan's go-ahead. How long it was suitable to keep that from them, she had no idea. She was beginning to think she should get in touch, but it was hard to know what to do when Nathan was stuck in a no man's land of existence.

Because Nathan had been asleep for so many days, they'd carried out a CT scan of his brain to check the surgery hadn't caused a stroke or something similar. Catatonic, they were calling it. That sounded far too scary to Emma. Like something they saved for movies; something that shouldn't be happening without a clapperboard declaring they were on take fifteen.

Emma closed the copy of the book she was reading. It was *The Beast in the Jungle* by Henry James. She wasn't sure why she'd picked it – the main character, John Marcher, believed he was destined to fulfil a catastrophic fate and waited for it intently. It was far too close to home for it to be suitable bedside reading for Nathan. She needed to source a jollier novel with a more upbeat tale. 'I don't think you were enjoying that book anyway,' she sighed. 'We'll have to make a start on something else.'

A noise escaped Nathan – not speech; more of a chirp. Like he was attempting to say a word, but all that was emerging was a strangled sound.

'What was that?' It was the first hint of life that Emma had witnessed since he'd returned from theatre, and she had to hold her breath to make sure she wasn't mistaken. Everything, even her own heart, was on pause. 'Say it again so I can hear properly.' She moved closer, her hand brushing against his skin. Never had she willed a sound to make itself known more. It didn't matter that it was just a noise. An incomprehensible chirp would be the sweetest sound she'd ever heard if it meant Nathan was still in there.

Emma wasn't beyond flopping her heart out onto a plate if it meant getting him back. 'Look, whatever idea you have in your head about dying, you have to let it go. You have to let go of all those fears and do whatever it takes to find your way back to us. I can't do anything to right the world without you here.'

Emma stopped talking in the hope Nathan might fill the interlude. Was it too much to hope that the one sound he'd emitted wasn't a fluke? Knowing her luck, she was making this speech on the back of a burp, and whatever hope was springing from her was the result of a gaseous bubble.

'We said we were in this as partners. We have our fertility appointment tomorrow. The next stage of this whole thing. This is the bit we do together. I don't know what to do without you.' Emma wasn't ready to lose him yet. She wasn't sure what she'd do without him, in more than one regard. This hadn't been on the cards. She'd not prepared herself for this kind of loss – one where his body was present, but the rest of him was not.

This was the moment where the clapper board should come in. The crew could reapply make-up, ready for a close-up. Ready for the moment when he would wake up and the happy reunion would happen. Nathan would suddenly be full of life and they would embrace and he'd say, '*I'm here for you,*' like there was nothing in the world to fear.

But there was nothing. Nada. Zilch.

If Emma thought shaking him awake would do any good, she'd do it, but she knew the medical staff had tried every trick and Nathan was undergoing every investigation to get to the bottom of it.

'I'm here for you.' Perhaps she wasn't the one that needed to hear that reassurance. 'I know I have treatment to come, but I'm still going to be here for you. Whatever happens, I'm going to make sure you're okay. Mum will too. We'll get through this together.' She wasn't able to say more, the toll of tears falling freely catching in her throat. She didn't want him to know she was crying.

No response.

She moved her glasses and brushed her tears away. Those were all the reassurances she was able to provide. There was so much that existed in the realms of the unknown, it was hard to know what to say. And sadly, the only thing Emma knew for certain was that tonight she would have to go home. Alone.

Chapter Twenty-Seven

'Any news, love?' The hope in her mother's voice was enough for her tears to start flowing once again.

Emma did her best to mop them up before going to the front room. 'No change,' she reported, in the same wooden way the nurses kept telling her.

'It's going to be okay, love. He'll come out of it at some point, and they'll let us know when he does. Go and get some rest. You've had another long day. I think we both need an early night.'

Carole was right. She was bone-weary after the uncertainty of the last few days. Even so, she was going to find it hard to sleep.

It broke her heart to go to bed with little hope that he was going to wake. With days of despair behind her, she'd not even had chance to contemplate what was to come.

For the first time, she'd found herself in love. It was ridiculous to think that it was something she'd waited for her whole life and here it had crept up on her in the most impossible of circumstances. Trust her to realise what it was only now that Nathan was out of reach. And because it wasn't the fairy-tale romance of her childhood dreams, the one she'd read over and over in all her treasured books, a kiss on the lips hadn't woken him up like it should have done. She knew because she'd tried it on her way out.

There was nothing for it other than to attempt to sleep. Like Nathan had told her before this, sometimes the only thing to do was to take what was happening one hour at a time. She would decide what to do about the appointment when she'd got some rest under her belt.

When the phone rang it startled her from the slumber she'd found herself in.

It was two in the morning.

No good phone call ever took place at that hour.

Chapter Twenty-Eight

Day Twenty-Four

'Where's Emma?'

Apparently Nathan had been asking the question on repeat since waking up at half one in the morning.

When Emma arrived at the ward, Nathan was up and dressed and pacing by his bed like a caged animal.

'There you are. I thought you were going to wait here?' Nathan brought her into a hug.

Emma responded with a great sense of relief finding its way to her pores and into her being. But there was an edge of caution. Something wasn't quite right.

'Has anyone spoken to you yet?' It was two thirty. Emma wasn't sure who would be about for Nathan to chat with.

'They keep telling me to wait by my bedside until the doctor gets here. I don't understand why I need to stay here when I've got you to take me home. They kept saying you weren't here and I didn't understand. But you're here now so that's good. We can go.'

It was apparent from Nathan's mumblings that he wasn't gauging everything from a fully rational perspective.

'You're not in the day surgery unit any more. They had to admit you as an inpatient. You didn't wake up as quickly as they'd hoped.'

'Excellent! A few bonus hours of snoozing. I don't see why we can't head home now though.'

It had been four days since Nathan's surgery, but it was clear he didn't have any concept of day or time. It was hard to know what to say to him. She would much prefer someone with some medical training to explain what had happened.

Emma peered at the nurse's station in the corridor in the hope of getting the attention of one of the staff. Surely someone should be speaking to Nathan and filling in the blanks.

One of the nurses noticed and popped over.

'The on-call doctor is on his way. They know Nathan is awake. Let us know if you need anything.'

A guide on how to cope in bizarre circumstances would have been good. Was it down to her to fill Nathan in on what had happened? She doubted the overnight nurse or the on-call doctor had the foggiest as to the strangeness of Nathan's unexplained unconsciousness.

For a second Emma let the relief wash over her and hugged him tight again. It was such a welcome feeling to hold him again, but at the same time it was foreign… This time Nathan was joining in less than she was. But even if he was a tad disorientated, at least he was once again conscious. And even if he didn't realise he'd been out of it for days, he did know who she was. They were huge doses of comfort to hold on to.

'What time is it?' It was taking a while, but it looked like Nathan might be coming to his senses, taking note of the closed curtains and dimmed lighting.

'It's two thirty in the morning,' Emma said, sounding like an exhausted mother who'd been woken up.

'Wow. That was quite a snooze.'

Emma wasn't sure what to say. She certainly didn't have all the medical jargon at her disposal to give a full and accurate explanation.

'What do you remember?' Emma didn't see the need for providing Nathan with traumatic footnotes if he didn't remember what had happened. If he had no recollection of waking up during the surgery, Emma didn't want to trigger the memory. That might even set him back into his non-responsive state. And she couldn't bear that – she had only just got him back.

'Going for surgery.'

Nathan made no mention of what had happened: the consciousness when he should have been unconscious; the unconsciousness when he should have been conscious.

'They're not going to let you out of the hospital in the middle of the night. We're going to have to wait here to see the doctor.' Emma managed to get Nathan to return to his bed space. He'd probably disturbed enough patients before she'd arrived.

'I'm not tired, though. What are we going to do?'

'Sleep. The only thing I want to do is sleep.' The turmoil of the last few days was catching up with her. The uncertainty had caused restless nights and now she was awake when she needed to play at being a patient again in a few short hours.

'Let's sleep then. Even if I don't need to, you can use my bed while we wait.'

The suggestion, although probably not in keeping with any hospital policy, was far too tempting to resist. It was a bed, and at that moment anything was better than nothing.

As Emma found her way under the covers, Nathan joined her. It was as intimate as she'd ever been with a man. There was barely room for the pair of them, so they had no choice but to snuggle close to one another.

Nathan gently stroked Emma's arm and the soothing sensation soon lulled her into the deepest sleep she'd ever had.

Only this was one she planned to wake up from.

She just had to hope Nathan did too.

Chapter Twenty-Nine

Emma was sick of appointments. That was why, for the first time in what felt like weeks, she was taking a trip to somewhere other than the hospital.

When the doctors finally saw Nathan, they hadn't been prepared to release him immediately, like he'd hoped. Instead, he needed to go for a few tests to confirm that his episode was well and truly over. He would be done by about four, when they were due to head to their joint appointment.

Instead of having Emma wait round (and she had been there from an exceptionally early time), the nursing staff had suggested she go home to have a rest and freshen up before returning later. She'd rested briefly, but now she was opting to spend some quality time with her mother.

'This isn't the right stop, is it?' Carole asked, as Emma pressed the button several stops earlier than usual.

'It is today.'

It was weird being this close to the library with no intention of going there. She'd been saved the task of having to speak to her boss thanks to her doctor's note, which meant he hadn't asked why she wasn't back at work yet.

'This way, Mum.' They didn't have far to go, and when they got there Emma gladly wheeled her mother's chair through the double doors.

'What's going on? What are we up to?'

'I thought we'd do something a bit different today. I figured we needed a treat.'

The waiter, the same one she'd seen before, showed them to their seats. Their table faced out to the courtyard, the tinkling noise of the fountain in the pond the only sound disturbing them.

'Isn't this beautiful? I never realised this hotel was big enough to have this hidden away.'

'I thought you'd like it.' Emma smiled. Ever since she'd been, she'd thought about how much her mother would love coming here. And how much she would love to bring her.

'It's wonderful. But what about Nathan? I thought we were on our way to see him?'

'I'm meeting him later this afternoon. Hopefully, he'll have been discharged and we'll go for our appointment. He was having some extra tests done today before being let out. They said there was no point me getting there early as he won't be on the ward. They said I should rest. This isn't quite resting, but it does seem like the perfect way to relax.'

Once they'd put in their order for afternoon tea, it didn't take long for it to be delivered. It looked every bit as good as Emma remembered, only this time they were skipping the champagne.

'Amazing.' Carole's eyes nearly popped out of her head at the selection on offer.

'Thank you, Mum, for everything.' Not so long ago, Emma would have thought this an impossibility. Maybe it would have been, if not for the courage her mother had gained when she'd taken flight with Nathan.

'I think I need to thank *you*, darling. You've done so much for me over the years. I think I have rather come to take it for granted. Now it's my turn to look after you as much as I can.'

Emma took her mother's hand. 'We can continue looking after each other. But not before enjoying afternoon tea. Shall I be mother?'

They'd stuck with the traditional choice of English breakfast tea. It had been made with loose tea leaves and Emma enjoyed the process of pouring it through the tea strainer before adding a splash of milk.

'This is such a treat. Can you dish me up one of those sandwiches?'

Emma popped a finger sandwich onto her mum's plate and helped herself to one as well. It was reassuring that it was so quiet in the hotel. If Carole had any spasms while eating, no one was going to sit and stare.

'I'm so glad we've come here. I came once before – the day I left work – because it all got a bit too much. It didn't feel right that you weren't here.'

It turned out that Carole jumping out of a plane had given Emma more courage to step outside her comfort zone as well. She was more capable than she would have ever believed. She just hoped she was able to keep hold of that thought in the coming weeks and months.

As they tucked into their cream cheese and cucumber finger sandwiches, it was a nice feeling to be doing something purely for pleasure.

It didn't take away from everything else that had been going on, but it was certainly a moment to enjoy. A slice of tranquillity while they were in the midst of a storm. The weight of the world could remain outside for now.

Fortunately, after all the tests that had been carried out, the doctors didn't find anything that made them want to keep Nathan in.

Emma had taken her mother home and then returned to the hospital, still full from the indulgent afternoon tea but ready for her appointment with Nathan. At least here it looked like they'd considered the design of their waiting room. There were pictures on the wall, all in shades of purple that subtly matched the paint. It didn't quite have the tea-and-coffee facilities she'd hoped for, but there was a water fountain, which was as close as she was going to get.

'Are you sure you're okay with us doing this?' Emma asked Nathan for approximately the 108th time.

She just needed to be sure. And it was really hard to be sure when the person she was asking had only just woken up from a three-day coma.

'They've told us if we freeze your eggs and my sperm separately, the chances are much lower. We don't know what the future holds, but by doing this together we're at least putting one set of odds in our favour. It makes perfect sense,' Nathan said. He'd clearly paid attention to the information pamphlet they'd been given.

Emma wished she had such conviction. Nothing seemed to make perfect sense at the moment.

'But what about after all this? What about five years from now, if we aren't in contact and we meet new people, and our only option is to have a baby with each other?' Emma was whispering, not wanting the staff to be aware that their next-of-kin status wasn't all it was made up to be. She didn't want to be a pessimist, but they needed to be pragmatic about this. It wasn't a decision to be made lightly.

'But we don't know what life will be like five years from now. We don't even know what it'll be like five months from now. All we know is what we have here and now, and if they're saying this gives us the best chance, we should take it.'

'This'll tie us together forever, you realise that?'

'Does it scare you?'

Lots of things scared Emma at that moment. The thought of Nathan falling asleep and not waking up again. Her surgery and how well it would go. Leaving her mother behind all alone. There were so many things to frighten her, yet the thought of having a baby with Nathan in the future didn't seem like one of them. Instead it sounded like a delightful impossibility. 'It doesn't scare me. I'm more scared about the possibility it might never happen.'

'In that case, let's go and make sure it can happen.'

Emma nodded in agreement. There were so many things to overthink, but this wasn't one of them. Who knew where they were going to be in the future? Letting their DNA forge together was for the purpose of preserving hope.

Whatever their future might hold, it should contain as much of that as possible.

Nathan's Diary

Ever since the surgery, I've been living in a fog. Things that are sup-posed to be straightforward have become complicated, and those that are simple have become complex.

While I was under, the dream continued on repeat. I kept hearing that baby crying over and over and like before, I still don't know what it means. What could it ever possibly mean?

But what they told us in the appointment – that a frozen embryo would have a greater chance of success in the future than if we were to freeze our eggs and sperm separately – that's when I knew.

I knew we should do it. We should create life and see where it takes us.

Chapter Thirty

Emma

Emma was doing her best not to get involved in the discussion between her mother and Nathan.

'Honestly, it's not a problem, and I'll have no further arguments over it. It works out for the best right now. We have to go with the solutions life presents us with.' Carole had been well and truly in charge over the past week.

'Only if you're sure. I don't want to intrude,' Nathan said.

'Stop worrying and go and put your bag upstairs.' Emma's mum pointed a finger that no one should argue with, even if it was trembling.

Without any help from Emma, over the past few days her mother had been sorting out everything she feasibly could to make life easier. She'd organised herself a morning and evening carer so the responsibility wouldn't fall to Emma. She'd finally got hold of her electric wheelchair and was learning to whizz through the house without the help of her daughter. She'd set up online shopping with the help of Emma's brother, who might not be good at visiting but was a technology whizz.

'How are you feeling, sweetie? Have a seat, would you?' It was like the front room had become a command centre from which her mother was going to take charge of everything.

Emma sat. Thankfully her bum wasn't hurting from the hormone injection.

'Are you sure this is okay? I know you've said it is, but I don't want to impose.' Nathan re-joined them, having deposited his bag, and sat next to Emma on the couch. His weight pulled her a little closer to him. It was good to have his warmth back.

'It's a vacant room. There's no way I'll be getting up there to use it. If your housemates aren't going to be any help while you're recovering, then it's better that you stay here. At least, between Emma and I, we can keep an eye on whether you're doing okay.' Carole moved her chair slightly, something Emma was yet to get used to.

Emma knew what her mother really meant was that they'd be around in case Nathan slipped back into a coma. As they hadn't worked out why it had happened in the first place, the doctors hadn't provided great reassurances over the likelihood of it not happening again.

'It's really good of you. Thank you,' Nathan replied.

'I don't think the doctors would have let you out without knowing someone would be around to keep an eye on you for the next couple of days,' Emma said. All of Nathan's flatmates worked full-time and none of them were able to drop work for anything less than a family emergency. Babysitting housemates didn't seem to count.

'Well, I'm glad to be here.'

'And we're glad to have you,' Emma's mother said.

She was right: Emma was glad too. After the worry of the past few days, it was reassuring to have him in the house, able to check on him as necessary.

It wasn't long before her mum's favourite game shows were on and not long after that her carer turned up. Nathan and Emma retreated upstairs. Emma felt a bit of a fraud, as she was perfectly well at the moment and would have happily sorted her mother's dinner and put her to bed.

'Are you okay if I come into your room? I feel weird just holing myself up in your mum's room.'

'Of course.' Emma tried to say it in a chilled manner, like she was used to having handsome men spending time in her bedroom.

She was suddenly acutely aware of every item she had in her bedroom, as if looking at them for the first time. Pebbles that she'd found at beaches and turned into paperweights; an entire shelf of notepads filled with unfinished poems and story ideas. Even the books said things about her that she might not have wanted anyone to know: her penchant for bird watching, for a start. But here they were on display, the intimate parts of her nature out on show. She hadn't realised that inviting someone into her own space would be quite so revealing.

Nathan started browsing the shelves. 'What book were you reading to me at the hospital?'

Emma sat on the edge of her bed, not entirely sure where to place herself in her own space now she had company. 'I didn't realise you knew I'd read to you. I didn't think you were awake.'

'I wasn't. I just thought you probably would have. Was it any of these?'

'No, I figured my tastes differed to yours slightly.'

'I never have spent enough time reading.'

There was an awkward silence for a couple of minutes while Nathan browsed the books on the shelves and Emma failed to find the right words. It wasn't easy when she wasn't sure what was going on between them.

'We should choose the name for your charity and get together a list of things we need to do.' Emma decided the best thing to do was to talk about something practical.

'And we need to sort out your trip to go and see puffins. We have to try and fit that in before you have surgery. You might not feel like it for a while after that. I can research it, if you like? Check how easy the travel will be and see if we can get the ball rolling.'

Knowing how quickly Nathan had got her mother into the air, Emma was pretty certain, if he put himself in charge of arranging something, it would happen soon. 'That would be great,' she said, still not sure what to say or how to act. So much had happened since their kiss. There was every possibility he might not even remember it.

Emma yawned. It was still early evening, but it wasn't a surprise to find that, after the past twenty-four hours, traces of exhaustion were beginning to show.

'You need to sleep and get some rest. I'll make sure your mum is okay. You have an early night,' Nathan said, noticing her tiredness.

There had been far too many shifts in who was the carer and who was patient in the past few days. She wasn't ready to take on the patient role yet, but Nathan was right about her needing to rest. The last few days had left her exhausted to her core.

'You need to rest too.' Not that Emma wanted to push him out of her room. 'You've been awake since three. You must be tired?' If there was any hope that Nathan was going to make a move on her, it disappeared as he made his way towards the door.

'I still feel strangely awake. I reckon I could go without sleep for another day or two. Being over-anaesthetised obviously comes with some benefits.'

'Not sleeping isn't a good thing.' Emma couldn't put her finger on it, but there was something different about Nathan since he'd woken up. There was an unease in his character she'd not noticed before. 'Come here.' She patted a space on the bed beside her. Maybe if they closed the gap between them, things wouldn't feel so strange.

Nathan hesitated for a moment, like he might take her up on her invite, but then thinking better of it, pulled away. 'You need to get your rest. I'll go and do some work. Because right now, not sleeping means not dreaming and I'm not going to miss doing that. Goodnight, Emma.' Nathan waved goodbye as he drifted out of her bedroom.

Her heart sunk. Was the Nathan she'd brought home from the hospital the same one she'd taken there only a few days before? He was quieter and somehow less engaged, his rebuffing of her invitation proof of that. He was moving in the same way and saying all the right things, but there was something missing.

Of course, if he had no memory of their kiss on the morning of his botched surgery, that might explain it. His body language didn't demonstrate any knowledge of their tryst. And so Emma was at a loss as to how to behave. They'd agreed to become parents together in the future, and yet she felt crushingly far apart from a man she'd felt so close to only a few days before.

The way he'd kissed her before they reached the hospital had her thinking he'd remove her clothes on the street given half a chance. This evening it was like such a thought had never existed in their lifetime. They were back to being strangers. United solely by their lumps.

Tiredness made Emma curl up into bed without changing into pyjamas or cleaning her teeth. Things like that seemed far too orderly and in keeping with normality. She felt neither of those right now.

She felt like she was stuck on the end of a parachute, but not with the wind gently guiding her in one direction. Instead it was pulling and shifting and pushing her this way and that. The responsibilities that were hers, the circumstances she never thought she would be in, the friendship that was more and yet not. All those strings and threads made her wonder if she was doing anything right.

It made her realise how a day had the power to change everything. That the things that could make somebody happy one moment might entirely shift and alter by the next. With each hour that passed, the landscape was changing. Sometimes, instead of never wasting an hour, she wanted to cling on to them so they wouldn't ever pass.

It was hard when the needs of each person in this house and Emma's life were altering.

Her mum had moved from an isolated woman to the person in charge.

Emma was no longer the carer, and soon she would need to be cared for.

Nathan had shifted from friend to something more, while, at the same time, something less. If only Emma wasn't too tired to establish what. It was a pity she wasn't able to stay awake, because who knew how much the landscape would change by morning.

Chapter Thirty-One

Nathan

There were sixty seconds in a minute.

There were sixty minutes in an hour.

The average adult human slept for seven to eight hours a night.

Nathan knew all these facts to be true.

He knew all these things because his brain had switched to hyperdrive. When they'd told him how long he'd been sleeping, it almost made sense because of the number of times he'd had the dream on repeat. Not once or twice, but a relentless cycle. It had been a never-ending whirr that wouldn't switch off, and in his comatose state his confused thoughts had continued. What did this recurring snippet mean? And why had it changed?

Sadly, his almost meditative state hadn't presented any answers. It had only fuelled his sense of concern. Right now he was trawling through the internet in the hope of shutting down some of those thoughts. He'd been doing it for more hours than anyone should in the middle of the night. It was an attempt to fill his head with noise while the rest of the house was quietly sleeping.

Being in someone else's bedroom wasn't helping. He didn't want to go raiding drawers in the hope of finding entertainment – not when that would entail looking through Carole's personal possessions. There were trinkets of jewellery on the dressing table, alongside half-finished embroidery projects. An unblinking doll peering at him as if he were doing something wrong.

And there it was again. It didn't take much to trigger the memory.

Even awake, the dream presented itself whole and uncensored. It was like it wanted to be felt. It didn't want to leave him.

Trying to make as little sound as possible, he grabbed a hoodie from his bag and threw it over the doll. The eyes were creeping him out and making him think of the last part of the dream. The new part. The baby crying. He'd taken it as a push towards deciding with Emma to have the fertility treatment. But what if, rather than encouragement, it was a warning?

Surely a man who'd been dreaming of his own death all his life should welcome this new variation? Surely a baby represented hope? A future that would continue even if he was gone. That was what he was trying to ensure happened, after all. But part of him was terrified.

Was the dream some kind of warning? The thought had been pulling at him for more hours than he cared to recall. Perhaps the dream had delivered the knowledge that he might die in order to make him pay more attention to the lump. Goodness knows how long he might have ignored the anomaly otherwise. And in the same way, perhaps the crying baby was a warning of a different kind. Maybe it was warning him not to risk becoming a father right now.

It was like chasing vapour trails. He was rational enough to know that none of it made sense. He just wasn't smart enough to work out what to do.

All he knew was that it was his ridiculous non-stop thinking that was preventing him from being snuggled up with Emma right now. He'd seen the look in her eye. He knew she'd wanted more than a cosy chat. If he got that close to her, he knew he'd want to do more than just talk as well.

And he had to put a stop to that.

He knew he was overthinking everything, but the dream, going over and over in his head, was stopping him from seeing straight.

However much he wanted to have children in the future, he didn't want to do anything to jeopardise the here and now. And because he'd been awake for too many hours, his imagination was in overdrive with the possibility of getting Emma pregnant.

Making love always held the potential to create life, and now that she'd started fertility treatment to allow the harvesting of her eggs, that chance would be even stronger.

That's why things had to stop. It was a decision. It was a responsibility. They couldn't risk doing something that might end up having consequences for Emma's health.

The noise was so clear in his head it was impossible to drown it out. He'd tried with various methods, but even the sound of his favourite band, the Smashing Pumpkins, wasn't working.

Inside his head there was a baby crying. Not a contented, happy cry. Not the gnarly cry of a baby that needed to be fed or burped or have its nappy changed.

It was the cry of a baby without a mother.

Nathan knew he couldn't sleep with Emma. Because if he did and she fell pregnant, he already knew who she'd choose to save.

She would stop treatment.

She would save the baby.

And he couldn't let that happen.

Nathan's Diary

It's amazing what you can get done in the wee small hours when it's impossible to sleep. I've been more productive in one night than I have in a long time. Anything to distract me, so that my thoughts don't drift to the dream.

I've looked into indoor skydiving and have decided I'll fund Rudi's first dip into the sport.

I've done everything I can from behind a laptop to get the ball rolling to set up a charity.

I've planned and booked Emma's trip to see puffins.

I have not yet ventured on to world domination. I don't think I'm ready for that in this lifetime, especially when my days are numbered. Besides, there's only so much you can do when everyone else is sleeping.

The point is, distraction is key at the moment.

Anything else means giving in to the reality…

Emma has cancer.

Pretty soon, I'm sure I'll find out I hold the same fate. Every day from now on is a blessing. I'm regarding nights without sleep as a precious gift of extra time – and time shouldn't be wasted.

Chapter Thirty-Two

Day Twenty-Eight

Emma

'Wake up! You need to pack your bags.'

Emma wasn't even out from under the duvet yet. She preferred to enjoy at least one cup of tea in the morning before talking to anyone. She normally made one on the sly before her mother woke up, sneaking it up to her bedroom to enjoy the combination of early morning caffeine and silence.

'What for?' Her voice was still a croak.

'Puffins.'

Not only did Emma need fluid on board to help operate her speech, she also needed food for her brain to function. 'What puffins?'

'Your wish was to see puffins in the wild. Soooooooooo...' Nathan said the word in that sing-songy way that demonstrated he was leading up to something special and obvious all at the same time.

Emma realised he was waiting for her to fill the gap. But that wasn't going to happen while she was in a state of shock. She wasn't even sure what day of the week it was. Or how many hours she'd slept. Or if she was behind on helping out with her mum. In fact, it had taken a few moments to remember why Nathan was there at all – in her house, in her room.

'We're going to see puffins in the wild!' Nathan said it with a startling amount of glee. Having reached a crescendo, his excitement hovered in mid-air as he waited for Emma to catch up.

Emma stared at him. It was too much to process when she was yet to fully let go of sleep.

'You do want to go and see puffins, don't you?' The deflation was already happening, the optimism in Nathan's tone already two decibels lower than it had been.

'Of course! But right now I'm not actually awake. I never am until I've had at least one cup of tea. I might be able to react once I've had my first cuppa.' Emma wasn't a morning person. No amount of Nathan's enthusiasm was going to change that fact. Having someone turn up like they were auditioning for the class of *High School Musical* did not inspire a sunny disposition in someone not yet ready to form words or thoughts.

'I'll go make tea. And breakfast. You wait there.'

Emma didn't plan on doing much else. It was all a bit overwhelming. She'd gone to bed feeling apprehensive, and an overly zealous wake-up call just added to the confusion. Even with Nathan's ethos of never wasting an hour, Emma liked to think there were some hours that were designed for resting and should be designated as such.

She felt strange this morning. Like somehow there were parts of her that weren't acting in the way she would normally expect. Perhaps it was the side effects of her hormone injection. Whatever it was, she felt a sense of uncertainty all over her body.

'Here we are,' Nathan chirped, as he returned to her room with a tray complete with a boiled egg and soldiers and her much-needed cup of tea. He nestled it onto her lap and perched himself on the edge of the bed next to her.

The thought of being told to pack her bags somehow filled her with dread… She still had her mother to consider. It was probably every girl's dream to hear that sentence, but right now she wanted nothing more than the comfort of home.

'Thank you,' Emma managed, after the first sip of tea. She really hadn't meant to be so impolite, but she wasn't used to such an assault on her senses so early in the day.

'Sorry, I thought you were awake when I came in. I didn't mean to scare you.'

'Just because someone's eyes are open, it doesn't mean they're all there yet,' she said with a smile. That was certainly the case for Emma's mum. Maybe not liking mornings was a genetic thing.

'Are you awake enough now?'

Emma took another sip of tea. It was barely enough caffeine to start an engine, but she would make the exception of only two sips, given that it was Nathan and she really shouldn't be reacting the way she was. 'I can form sentences. Is that a hopeful sign?'

'That'll do. So, I looked into it last night. If we go to the Bempton Cliffs reserve site, which is looked after by the Royal Society for the Protection of Birds, we stand a reasonable chance of seeing a puffin, and Yorkshire is the closest place to go. We can do the trip in a couple of days. It's a bit of a trek on the train, so we could stay a bit longer if you're happy to. If we go today, it should work out okay with your tablets and injections.' Nathan looked particularly wired, saying each sentence so fast it was almost impossible to keep up.

'Have you had any sleep?'

'Not really.'

'I can kind of tell. Aren't you exhausted?'

'Anything but. Sorry if I've woken you up with too much enthusiasm. You must be tired. Do you think you're up to doing anything?'

Emma wasn't quite awake enough to know how she was feeling. She normally saved judgement until she was at least standing. 'It sounds wonderful. And as long as I don't need to be ready in ten minutes then I should be okay.' She started to tuck into her food. She wasn't going to let it go cold when it might be another millennium until she was brought breakfast in bed again.

The egg yolk was in a perfect oozy state, dribbling out as she dunked in a soldier. The sight only made her hungrier, so she figured she wasn't harbouring a tummy bug in her state of not feeling right. 'Did you make yourself some?' Emma felt a bit self-conscious eating with someone watching.

'Just for you and your mum. I ate some toast while I was waiting for the eggs to boil.'

The thought that her mother was also enjoying this service made Emma smile. It also reminded her why she wasn't able to just up and leave on random missions, even to see a puffin in the wild. 'I can't just leave. Someone needs to be here for her.'

'I've talked to her about it. She has her carers coming in regularly now and she's called someone to come and stay with her. They should arrive later today. She's happy for us to go on the trip together. In fact, she's encouraging it.'

Emma chewed on a toasted soldier so as not to have to answer straight away. It was like she was being ganged up on, although it wasn't exactly a punishment they were dishing out. It was her everlasting act. Perhaps that was why she wasn't jumping for joy… She wasn't ready for anything to be final yet.

'Who's coming to stay with Mum?'

'Your brother.'

'Really?' It had been so long since James had done anything useful, she'd forgotten that he might be capable of such feats.

'Really. I don't think your mum gave him a choice. Are you going to come?'

'I haven't got any reason not to.' It wasn't exactly the full-on cheering that perhaps Nathan had been hoping for, but she wasn't about to reel off excuses as to why she wasn't able to go. She'd spent far too much of her life not living. She wasn't going to miss out on an opportunity like this – especially when it was presented to her fully organised, without her having to lift a finger. 'Let me eat breakfast and get dressed and I'll come down to talk to Mum about it.' She wanted to make sure her mother was happy for herself.

Admittedly, it was rushed, and she knew that was the reason for her hesitation. Perhaps she was close to being in shock. Having breakfast in bed was revelation enough for one morning.

Puffins were bound to bring about happiness, though. She had enough well-thumbed books which she'd read while daydreaming about the possibility. Freedom from her responsibilities would also do her some good. But for some reason there was a glossy film fogging her view and preventing her from being joyful about the whole thing, and she wasn't able to fathom why that was.

Some days it was harder than others to paste on a mask and pretend everything was okay. Today, not even warrior paint would cover over the cracks that life was providing.

Chapter Thirty-Three

Nathan

Nathan tucked the dream diary away in his overnight bag. If anyone read it, they'd think he was losing his mind. He couldn't be entirely sure he wasn't, what with the lack of sleep. There wasn't enough coffee in the world to sort him out at the moment.

Emma was sleeping right now, the train's movement lulling her into slumber. Nathan wished it would do the same to him. He'd never reached this level of overtiredness, to the point where he didn't know what to do with himself. If it carried on, he'd have to ask the doctors for sleeping pills.

What he wouldn't do to be resting his head on Emma's shoulder in a similar state of shut-eye. But, for whatever reason, his body wasn't allowing him to rest, and he wasn't about to risk waking her while she slept so peacefully. Plus, he probably shouldn't get that close.

With every train change, Nathan had to deal with the guilt of waking her, but then she would fall asleep again on the next leg of the journey. It was clear this wasn't just the result of traveller's fatigue. Whatever hormone cocktail had entered her veins yesterday was clearly taking its toll.

As they passed beautiful landscapes – horses in paddocks, wide rivers and fields beginning to blossom – he really hoped he'd done the right thing. He'd had this awful sense that there would never be another right time. For the first time, he was recognising that perhaps it wasn't the healthiest way to go about life. Maybe if he'd waited a couple of days, Emma wouldn't have been so tired and would have taken more of this in. And he was yet to see how she would cope over the next couple of days. He was going to have to take it hour by hour and let her rest as much as she needed.

There was another reason why he was worried. There were certain things it was impossible to have an influence over, and there was no way he could change what season they were in. And the season meant there was every chance they wouldn't even see a puffin.

It was all very well chasing dreams, but it was never easy to accept they might not be there to be captured.

But Nathan being Nathan, he vowed to do his best no matter what.

Chapter Thirty-Four

Emma

If Emma had required tea to wake her that morning, now she needed some matchsticks to hold her eyes open. Every opportunity they got they were closed, and every time Nathan woke her, she was less sure of their location.

Nathan was keeping her informed, but the facts went whistling off with the wind. The moment she had hold of a place name it had whipped away and they were somewhere else.

'We're nearly there. Only a few more stops.'

Nathan shook Emma into some kind of consciousness for the umpteenth time, to get them off the train. She'd lost count of how many times she'd been woken. 'Where are we?' They might be returning to Timberley Drive for all she knew, rather than heading north-east, up and across the country towards Yorkshire.

'We've made it to our final destination. We're in Bempton. I'll get us a taxi to the cottage. We'll visit the RSPB Bempton Cliffs reserve tomorrow. It's too late for us to travel there today.'

Emma nodded. She really was being the worst company ever, but little had she known the effect one injection would have on her.

At least she was only sleepy. Travelling would have been a whole different ball game if she was chucking her guts up.

In the taxi, Emma rediscovered the ability to keep her eyes open. Bempton flashed by in a whizz of picturesque white houses and idyllic green pastures. They stopped at a place that was directly opposite a church and graveyard. It was late, but the scene was brought to life by a floodlight that cast shadows where she would rather there weren't any.

Nathan paid the taxi driver and Emma realised she hadn't given him a penny yet. All of this – the train journey and the accommodation – must have been paid for already. 'You need to let me know what I owe you for all this. This is my everlasting act, after all.'

'Let's not worry about that. We should get inside in the warm.' Nathan started fiddling with what Emma recognised to be a key safe: a small box on the wall that required a code to be opened. There was one back at her own house so the carers had access to a key when they visited.

Emma followed Nathan into the small cottage, which was deceptively large once inside. Despite being pretty much an open-plan bedsit, it was a really fancy one. The part that made it larger than it seemed was an extension that had perhaps been a pig shed at some point. It had no conventional windows and from the outside it didn't appear to belong to the same building, but once inside it was the part that housed the bed area. The absence of normal windows was made up for by a skylight.

The front door opened straight into a lounge which had an open kitchen. Emma ventured in, peering in cupboards and behind doors, getting familiar with the surroundings. There was one separate room that housed a shower and toilet. Peering outside, she saw that there was a perfectly formed courtyard. If it hadn't been so cold, it would have been just right for sitting out to enjoy the evening sun. It was a magical little hideaway; Emma was sure she would never have found something quite so quaint and wonderful at such short notice. There were even books on the shelves, some of which she had at home, like a nod to it being exactly the kind of place she should stay.

'Where did you find this place?' she asked.

'I found it on Airbnb. I thought you might like it.'

'It's gorgeous,' Emma said, giving the place a once-over again.

And before she'd even seen a puffin, Emma felt it happening – a smile spreading across her face. Like this was meant to be happening and she was meant to be here.

There were just two things worrying her.

First, she wasn't ready to die anytime soon. The fact she'd listed this as her last act was making her nervous. There was no way she wanted that to be how it actually worked out.

Second, there was only one bedroom. With one bed. It was going to be very hard not to overthink exactly what that meant. The only thing to do was to wait until bedtime…

Chapter Thirty-Five

Way before bedtime, Emma's main concern was her mounting hunger. She couldn't remember having food since breakfast, and travelling had taken the best part of eight hours. She'd slept through lunch as they'd trundled across the country on the train.

'I'm starving. Is there any food about?' she asked, deciding that it was a better idea to concentrate on things she did have a handle on.

There was a tray in the kitchen with supplies for the usual beverages, and there were a couple of wrapped biscuits there, but they weren't going to scratch the surface of her current appetite. She'd been the worst company for Nathan since the moment he'd woken her up that morning, and she didn't want to add 'hangry' to the list of unlikeable qualities she'd been demonstrating.

'There's a fish and chip shop about a five-minute walk from here. I can wander down there and hope that it's open. If not, there are a couple of takeaway places not far away that should deliver here.'

'Did you really research all of this in one night?' It was hard to believe only yesterday this hadn't been on their agenda.

Nathan shrugged. 'Food is important. I wanted to make sure we weren't too far out in the sticks, especially as we didn't drive and couldn't load up the boot with food on our way.'

'Fish and chips it is then.'

'What do you want?'

'I'll come with you. I could do with the fresh air to wake me up – I haven't been this sleepy for a long time. And I can't have you getting lost in a strange village.'

It was an excuse to be with Nathan. She'd spent far too much of the day absent. She wished she had spent more time awake, not wanting to miss out on a single part of her adventure.

It was strange to be somewhere so much more scenic than what she was used to at home. Here there were a pub and post office at the centre of the village, creating a cosy feel, with not much else apart from picture-perfect houses and stunning views across the rolling countryside. She knew that every town and village was different, each with its own little nuances, but so often she saw them in TV programmes or online or imagined them in the books she read. It was quaint to be in a place that had a noticeboard with leaflets about craft groups and upcoming fairs right in the middle of the street.

It was strange walking with Nathan – side by side, not arm in arm. The natural ease that had once been between them seemed to have vanished into thin air.

It was amazing how a three-centimetre gap was a chasm neither of them was able to cross. What made it harder was that Emma wasn't sure if Nathan wanted her to. Even though they'd shared a kiss, there had been no mention of it since Nathan had woken up. Emma inched half a centimetre closer. She wanted to think of a question, something to get the conversation flowing without forging into awkward territory. 'Have you come up with a name for your charity yet?'

'I've had a few ideas. Some of them sound a bit cheesy though. I thought about "Foxdale Flights", but it sounds too like a new airline. I kind of need something that reflects its purpose.'

They reached a crossroads and turned a corner. Up ahead was the neon sign of a chip shop. It really was only a five-minute walk away, if that. And the fact the sign was lit gave her much hope that soon they would have sustenance.

'Right, what would you like to have?' Nathan asked.

One of everything off the menu seemed a little greedy, but Emma was so ravenous she'd have a good shot at seeing her way through the order. 'My eyes might be bigger than my belly, but can I order fish and chips with a battered sausage on the side?'

Perhaps one of the side effects of the injections would be becoming the size of a house. She was sure she would if her appetite was this shouty all the time, but the wafts of salt and vinegar along with frying fish were making it stronger. For now, she was going to put it down to the fact she was making up for missing out on a meal.

Nathan was more reserved in his ordering and went for a steak and kidney pie and chips. They weren't waiting long, as they were the only customers in the shop. Their food was wrapped up in paper and Emma appreciated the fact that at least the hormone injection wasn't making her desire a pickled onion on the side.

Once they were walking back, Emma made a conscious effort to close the gap and keep the conversation flowing.

'What about calling it The Nathan Foxdale Trust?'

'It certainly has a ring to it, but doesn't that make it sound like I've gone already? Like it's been set up in memory of me?'

'I guess. And hopefully we'll both be around once it's officially set up.' Emma really hoped so, and wished Nathan would start to believe it as well.

'What about Everlasting Acts?' said Nathan. 'I like the idea that it's what started this whole thing in the first place.'

'Yes! That way it can be for other things too. It can fund simple trips like this one for people who aren't daredevil enough to jump out of aeroplanes.'

'Yeah, so it's more of an *us* idea… Like how this whole thing started.'

Emma's cheeks flushed with pride. The idea that something good was going to come out of this filled her with a new sense of purpose. To go with the 'us', Emma decided to link arms with Nathan. It was an offer of support and a step towards no longer feeling awkward in his presence.

There was no smooth way of making such a manoeuvre though, especially when she was thinking about it so consciously. But then, what happened to never wasting an hour? It was time to be brave. Emma went for the lunge. It was like she was a clumsy teenager again – though, really, had she ever graduated from that phase? Nathan had been her first kiss. Managing not to fall over her own feet, Emma linked her hand through his arm, the bag of food dangling between them. She wasn't sure what kind of reaction she'd been hoping for. One not dissimilar to when they'd first kissed, perhaps. That sense that he would rip her clothes off in five seconds given half a chance. As it was, he didn't even switch which hand the bag was in to stop the food from banging her leg.

'Are you okay?' She didn't know what else to ask. What other question was there that would help unlock why he'd changed without unlocking everything he'd been through.

Nathan took hold of Emma's hand and held it briefly before letting go. 'We can't be a thing. I've been thinking about it a lot, and it just can't happen.'

They weren't far from the graveyard now. Only a hundred metres or so and they would be outside the church, with their little cottage across the road.

Emma's heart sank towards her knees as she ground to a halt. She stared at Nathan for a moment, wondering what had prompted his change of heart.

There was no one around, but Emma was embarrassed and hurt by the public declaration. It might only be the souls stranded in the churchyard who bore witness, but still it was a hard thing to hear.

'Fair enough,' Emma said, trying not to let her feelings reach the surface. Not wanting to think on it further, she started to close the distance towards the cottage.

'I didn't mean that I don't want to – I do – it's just…'

Emma wasn't listening. She was too busy concentrating on putting one foot in front of the other. It was good to concentrate on something physical to stop the imminent tear leakage that was threatening.

She should have trusted her instincts. She'd known something was different. She'd sensed it since he'd woken. Perhaps he'd moved on to the next woman he wanted to get with.

The cottage and what had felt like a once-in-a-lifetime romantic trip were obviously just because he felt sorry for her and the cancer treatment she was facing. It was all to do with wanting to carry out her everlasting act and nothing to do with any feelings he had for her.

Those had gone along with his lump.

Chapter Thirty-Six

There wasn't anywhere for Emma to hide her upset, however much she tried. Rushing to the cottage was all very well and good, but she'd not thought ahead enough to realise she wasn't in possession of a key. And she'd not rushed off quick enough, because Nathan was still keeping up with her.

'Look, I'm sorry. I shouldn't have blurted that out like that. I need to explain.' Nathan rested the palm of his hand on the small of her back.

Automatically, Emma flinched away. 'You've made yourself quite clear.' She didn't need to hear the reasons he wasn't attracted to her. She needed to focus on herself, and right at that moment that meant eating above all else. 'I need to eat.' If the only sausage action she was getting was of the battered variety, then she wanted to enjoy it.

He let them in without saying anything more and Emma raided the small kitchen area to find plates and cutlery. Following her lead, Nathan helped dish up the food. Between them they got everything ready and laid out on the small dining table that was tucked neatly against the wall in the lounge. Emma realised all it needed was a candle to be the perfect tribute to a romantic moment.

It was as far away from that as possible. It was just Emma's luck that being whisked away – the most romantic gesture ever carried out for her – had absolutely nothing to do with Cupid. Instead, it was a friend making sure she got to do stuff before her treatment got too much. Or the cancer took over.

'I want to explain,' Nathan said, as Emma tucked into her first chip.

It was a big chip. Not one that was easily navigated without choking to death if she tried to talk.

'It's not that I don't want to. I think you're one of the most unexpected delights to have come into my life. I've never known someone so beautiful and selfless. But something has changed.'

If Emma hadn't been so busy with her food, she would have sung 'la-la-la' and stuck her fingers in her ears. She didn't need to hear why she was wonderful and also why she wasn't in one statement. Swallowing down the last of the chip, she was able to put up a protest. 'Honestly, you don't need to explain yourself. It's fine. We don't have to talk about it.'

There were so many explanations running through Emma's mind – everything from him having caught something unsavoury from one of his exes to realising he didn't find her attractive and now considered their kiss a mistake. She didn't need confirmation as to which was correct.

Nathan hadn't started eating yet. It wasn't going to stop Emma from digging in. She was ravenous. That in itself was enough to make her want to cry.

'I need to tell you, but it's going to sound crazy.'

That was a good description for everything that had happened these past few weeks. She was beginning to think nothing would surprise her, but then there was every possibility that thinking that was about to jinx her. She allowed a pause between mouthfuls. 'Go ahead with the crazy.'

'It's to do with the dream.' There was hesitation in his voice. 'It's changed.'

Emma knew that what he was saying mattered. It didn't make sense, but rather than grabbing another chip, she put her hand halfway across the table. If he wanted something to hold, it was there. She wasn't going to make the mistake of going all the way again, only to be rebuffed like she had been outside, but it was a gesture to show she was a friend and was there to listen if he needed to be heard. 'Go on.'

'I don't even know what to make of it. The change, that is.' Nathan took her hand and studied it for a while, like it would help.

'What is it?' Emma encouraged.

Nathan stared at his uneaten pie with a bone-shatteringly tired gaze. 'You know how I've always thought this would be the year that I die? Because of the dream I keep having?'

It was such a crystallising thought. 'Have you had your results?' Emma wanted to chastise herself for not asking the question before. If he'd had the results while he was still at the hospital, of course his behaviour would have changed. Why hadn't she thought to ask before?

'No. They won't be through until we're back in Salisbury. It's not to do with that. It's to do with the dream.'

'What about it?'

'It's changed. At first I thought it was a mistake and I'd heard something in my sleep, but it keeps happening. Every time I sleep I hear the same thing.'

'Hear what?'

'Most of the dream is the same as it was. I'm in a hospital room, I'm struggling to breathe, there's someone there and I'm not sure who it is.'

'So what's different? What do you hear?'

'There's a baby crying. Now every time the dream finishes, there's a baby crying.'

'Oh.' It was as abstract as the rest of the dream. Emma didn't understand. Weren't dreams just our daytime fears coming to haunt us? Certainly that's what her dreams tended to be. Whatever was troubling her was sure to crop up at night. Maybe Nathan had some kind of fear of becoming a father. 'What do you think it means?'

Nathan held onto her hand tighter. 'I wish I knew. I realise it might be nothing, but I keep coming back to the fact that all of it must have some significance. Why would I dream it otherwise? I've had a while to think about this, and every time I hear that baby, I'm almost sure it's part of me.'

'And if it is?' Maybe Nathan was having second thoughts about them creating an embryo together. She would understand if he were.

'At first I thought the dream was a way of encouraging me to preserve my fertility. But now I think the dream's a warning.'

'A warning about what?' Emma poked another chip in her mouth. The timing might not be perfect, but she needed nourishment.

'It's not that I don't want us to get close. I'm just freaking out, and I know I'm getting ahead of myself… But I'm just worried that, you know, if we get too intimate… I'm worried I'll get you pregnant.'

Emma did actually choke on the chip a bit this time. She'd not signed up for an immaculate conception quite yet. 'I think we're both adult enough to know there's protection to prevent that.'

In a way, she felt relieved. She'd been filled with worry over what she'd done wrong, but it was just a dream stopping Nathan. Something that was nothing to do with her. But the knowledge of that didn't stop the hurt driving its way into her, and she wasn't able to look directly at him.

Nathan raked a hand through his hair, as if getting hold of his roots might ground him somehow. 'But protection isn't one hundred per cent effective. Nothing is a complete fail-safe. There's only one way we can stop it happening. We don't need any unexpected babies. Not right now. I know that sounds harsh, but we need to keep you healthy.'

For the first time in Emma's life, she was gobsmacked. She'd been close to it a few times – the closest being the time a book was returned to the library with brown stains on most pages which, judging by the smell, well, it wasn't chocolate. But that hadn't left her literally speechless, unable to form any words. What Nathan had just said, Emma was struggling to understand.

'Let me get this right… Your dream now involves a baby crying, and you've interpreted that as a reason for us not to have sex? If, indeed, that was on the cards – which, right now, was a big assumption on your part.'

'I know it sounds daft. But you couldn't have chemo if you were pregnant. And I figured with the fertility treatment they've started you on it might be even riskier. You'll be more fertile. Emma, you have to understand, I've had this dream so many times. Almost every night for my whole life. I know it's going to come true. And I can't help but think it's a warning. It's been driving me mad thinking it over. I just don't understand what it means otherwise.'

There were many things Emma had thought Nathan might say, but this was so far removed from any of them she didn't know quite what to make of it.

'What else has your dream stopped you doing?' There was an anger rising in Emma.

'What do you mean?'

She pushed her chair back, wanting to distance herself from the insult. 'Exactly that. What else has this dream stopped you doing? In all these years, when you've been having that dream on repeat, what have you decided to *not* do because of it?'

'Well, nothing.'

'So in all those years it didn't stop you doing anything?' It was hard to fathom how maddening the statement was.

Nathan shrugged, as if what he was saying was logical and made some kind of sense. 'If anything, it did the opposite. It made me do all the things I was scared of.'

'But now it's made you scared of something. *Me.*' There was hurt trailing through Emma's words that she'd not meant to let loose.

'Not you.'

'Then what? If you've spent every moment taking every risk that life has to offer, why would you worry about it now? Why would the very slim possibility of creating life scare you?' Emma was letting hurt and anger cascade out of her like a waterfall.

'Because I'm scared of losing *you.*'

'Well, you're losing me either way! It's a dream, Nathan. That's all it is. Nothing should govern your entire life, especially something that isn't true. The dream shouldn't have any bearing on you. On us. It only does because you're letting it.'

'But if it's not true, why do I keep having it?'

It was a bit too much when she was hurting, exhausted and hungry. She didn't have any of the qualifications required to answer Nathan's question.

'People have recurring nightmares. It only matters because you're hanging onto it.' Emma stood up.

'I've never known what to do about it.'

Emma lifted her plate. She needed to get away, even if the only place to escape to was the bathroom. And she was taking the chips with her. 'I'm not sure I'm the person to help you. At least not today.'

'Don't go. We need to talk some more.'

But Emma was already gone.

As she sank down onto the bathroom floor, feeling like a fool, she thought that perhaps she might have come up with a better plan. But she was too hungry to concern herself with the hygiene particulars of eating in the same room as the toilet.

It didn't make her feel much better though; only less hungry.

'Emma,' Nathan said through the bathroom door. 'You can't stay in there all evening. I'll sleep on the sofa. We can go back first thing tomorrow.'

'Will you shut up? I just need the chance to think.'

There were certain occasions when thinking was such a crucial thing to do. People didn't do enough of it. Those thoughts would end up bringing about actions, and those actions would have consequences. Right now, Emma needed to think about consequences, because what she did next would really matter.

Nathan was having a recurring dream that was affecting his actions. It wasn't quite voices in his head telling him what to do, but all the same, he was listening to the dream above all else, beyond the point of reason.

Sometimes, for all the thinking in the world, there were no obvious answers. One man's dream was another man's madness. Emma was no longer worried about getting to grips with what stage their relationship was at; she was more worried about Nathan and how a dream was dictating his life. They already had a reality that was tough enough to deal with. They didn't need the fiction his dream was creating adding to that heavy load.

Chapter Thirty-Seven

Nathan

There was nothing Nathan could do other than respect Emma's wishes and give her the peace and quiet she required. He knew his explanation sounded crackers. Her response was confirmation of that fact.

With nowhere to go inside the cottage that would give Emma the space she needed, Nathan had to come up with another plan.

'I'm going out,' he said to the closed bathroom door.

Once he left, he wasn't sure what to do with himself. He really was tired. Finally, his sleepless night was catching up with him. Realising he didn't have the energy to embark on a long trek, he crossed the road to the churchyard in the hope of finding a bench – somewhere to rest his weary soul.

This wasn't how any of this was meant to be going. He loved Emma. Having never experienced it before, he was at a loss as to how to convey how he felt. He wanted her to know that he loved her, but somehow everything he did was making him look like a prize idiot.

Who fell in love with someone and did everything they could to make them happy, but also kept them at arm's length? To protect what, exactly?

The crying baby had only appeared in his dream a short while ago, and yet the puzzle of what it meant had consumed him. He had utterly convinced himself that it meant he would get Emma pregnant, and the potential consequences of that were too painful to consider. It seemed easier to just decide they should never have sex. He hadn't even stopped to consider whether that was what Emma wanted.

Circling the church with the wind against him, it seemed that no one round here ever required a bench to sit on, so instead Nathan opted for a sheltered patch of grass near the grave of someone called Doris Moore.

He was glad it was only the wind battering him and not rain. 'I hope you don't mind me intruding on you like this, Doris. I just need a quiet spot to think.' Nathan wasn't sure on the etiquette of graveside conversation. On the one hand it seemed a tad inappropriate; on the other, he was probably the first company Doris had had in years.

'A lot has happened to me recently,' he said, as if Doris was somehow listening. 'I've always thought my life was going to change when I turned twenty-seven. Most people would be looking forward to getting married or having a kid at my age, but here's me with a complex about dying. A bit young, I realise, but I've always known that this is the year that will be my last. The one in which I die. Did you have any inkling? Like before *you knew*, did you somehow know?'

There was a patch of clover in the grass by Doris's grave. Nathan wove his hand through them, trying to spot one with four leaves. He needed to find something that would bring him good luck. 'I don't think it's the norm for anyone to know. Okay, fair enough, it might be different if you have a diagnosis or you're given a life expectancy, but to know before you know those things – that's not the average experience, is it?'

It was eerie in the graveyard, with only the floodlight from the church illuminating the outside space. It summoned shadows where there was nothing to see and created images that weren't there. If Nathan's imagination was as strong as what he produced at night, he could well invent the ghost of Doris sitting next to him. At least he knew she wasn't going to answer anytime soon. He had to hope not anyway.

'And I don't think it's the norm to let dreams affect the way you act either?'

Doris wasn't answering, even though Nathan left a pause. A tree creaking in the wind made him wonder if some other spirits wanted to wade in on the conversation. It was enough to make him pull his coat tighter around him.

'I don't suppose I've ever thought about it in the right way. I wonder how the rest of the world would react if, when they were born, they got to know when they would die? Hopefully not everyone would behave like me. Hopefully there would be some people who would act a little kinder. Do something a bit more worthy than I have. I'm not even sure why I chose this hedonistic whirl of a life.'

Nathan moved his head nearer to the clover patch, ignoring the chilly blast of the wind. He hoped a closer inspection might yield a lucky shamrock, but the light was too poor to even attempt to find one.

'I think it's because I was trying to prove the dream wrong. Almost willing myself to die at a younger age so it wasn't right. What kind of twisted, messed-up thinking is that, Doris?'

The markings on Doris's grave weren't clear enough to work out how old she was when she died. How long her life had been was impossible to tell. But what did the dates matter? Nathan was sure he'd read a quote somewhere that the important bit was the dash in-between and all the days it represented. How many they would be was impossible to know. Even with the notion that he would die at the age of twenty-seven, he had no idea on which of the 365 days it would happen. He should be making the dash count, not obsessing over the end point.

'And here I am getting it all wrong again. How has a baby crying in a dream ended up changing what I do in life? If I do end up creating life, is that really such a bad thing? And if it's with Emma – the woman I've fallen in love with – would that be so wrong?'

Nathan used both hands for the four-leaf-clover hunt, as if this patch of land would grant him the luck the rest of life was depriving him of.

'You see, the problem is I've never worked out the reason for the dream. I feel like it must have a purpose, and the puzzle is working out what that is. I've always just regarded it as a warning. It's been telling me that this is what's going to happen, so make the most of your life. Do everything you can to make your life whole. Funny, isn't it? How when you get closer to the end it's anything but – how you see what you've been missing and where you've gone wrong. Do you know what I mean, Doris?'

It was hard to know if Doris would have had these same thoughts. Would anyone live their life like Nathan had? 'I just wish I'd done something a bit more fulfilling with it all, you know? Hopefully I'm not leaving it too late with the idea of setting up this Everlasting Acts charity.'

It was getting colder, and the light wasn't much help on Nathan's clover hunt. It was time to give up and move on, like he should have done a while ago. If he wasn't welcome inside the cottage, he'd have to find the nearest pub with the help of his phone. As he checked his pockets, he realised he must have left it behind.

He wasn't ready to move quite yet though. He didn't want to leave without giving Doris the whole story.

'You see, the thing is, they found a lump. It's gone now – they've taken it. But it's not as simple as that, is it? They have to make sure you're safe – make sure nothing is destined to return. And I do wonder, what even is the point? Is there any point in prolonging the agony if I know it's going to finish me all the same?'

Nathan hugged his coat around him, knowing it was time to move whether he wanted to or not. The wind was freezing his limbs solid, and if he didn't thaw soon, his senses might never return.

'It's been nice talking to you, Doris. It's a relief to be able to say things out loud and not worry about the weight of those words or what it'll make you think of me.' It was mad to think that even though his dream was one of the most affecting parts of his life, he rarely spoke to anyone about it, confiding only in his dream diary. Emma was the first person he'd ever been fully frank with, but being frank had hurt her feelings. What a mess. 'I hope we get to meet on the other side, wherever that is.'

'Nathan!'

The sound of his name nearly made him trip as he was attempting to get up. He sure as hell hoped Doris hadn't turned up to make their union occur earlier than he wanted. He wasn't ready to play at being a ghost just yet.

But he knew there was only one person around here who would be calling his name.

'Nattthhhaaannn!'

Emma was shouting from the doorway of the cottage, and if his intuition was still intact despite the cold, he was pretty sure the cry was edged with a touch of fear.

Moving as fast as he was able to while shivering, Nathan responded to Emma's call. 'What is it?' he asked when he reached her.

'The hospital's been trying to call you. I think it's urgent.'

Chapter Thirty-Eight

Of course Nathan knew the hospital was trying to get hold of him. He'd been trying his very best to ignore that fact. Whatever level of urgency they deemed the results to have, he'd decided not to let it affect the time he was spending with Emma. Although he was doing a fairly good job of ruining that himself.

Standing in the light of the doorway, Emma looked exceptionally cute in an oversized woollen jumper, a panicked flush colouring her cheeks.

'Thank fudge you're okay. Are you coming in?'

Nathan smiled. He didn't know anyone else polite enough to use 'fudge', when he was sure another F-word would be on the lips of most other people he knew. 'If I'm welcome?'

Emma waved him in. She was clearly cold. If the jumper wasn't enough to give that away, the fact she was shivering definitely was.

'Why didn't you tell me?'

'What do you mean?'

Even though Emma seemed cold, her reception was so far warmer than what he'd been hoping for. He just didn't want to walk straight into another argument. They'd done enough of that already this evening.

'Why haven't you told me that the hospital wants to see you? That you should be there, not here?'

'I didn't know that. Not for sure.' He'd suspected, maybe. When they'd been travelling earlier, he'd opted to ignore the call. He hadn't wanted to wake Emma when she needed sleep, and he thought if it were especially important they'd leave a message.

Instead they'd rung again. And again. 'How do you know?' It suddenly occurred to him that, as he wasn't certain of its importance, he wasn't sure how Emma could be.

Emma passed him his phone. 'There's a text message from your cancer support nurse. It sounds pretty urgent. You should call them.'

'We need to warm this place up. That's what we need to do right now.' It was as cold in their accommodation as it had been in the graveyard.

'We need to go home.'

'Do you want to go home?' Nathan wouldn't blame her if she did. He'd been far too cold and distant with her, and on top of that the place was like an ice cube.

'No, I don't mean that. I mean you need to get back to the hospital.'

Nathan could hear Emma's frustration – like reasoning with him was becoming a complete and utter impossibility. How did he even begin to explain?

'Look, it's late. We're not going anywhere tonight, and there's no way we should leave without doing what we came here to do. There's no point in us having travelled this far if we don't attempt to see some puffins tomorrow. Doing that's not going to change anything.'

There was a wood-burning stove, and Nathan started to tackle it – adding kindling and paper and making a cosy nest, ready to light. 'Whether I call them today or tomorrow or the next day, it's not going to change what the results are. My life isn't going to improve by rushing to find out what I already know.'

'But you don't know yet, do you? You don't know what they'll want to do or when your treatment might need to start.'

The kindling started to spark and Nathan nursed the flames to ensure the fire caught and would keep going for the rest of the evening. 'I know it's not good news. You do too. We both know the hospital wouldn't be chasing me if it was to award me with a hamper for being a good patient. We should embrace the not knowing while we can.'

'But what if they need to book you in for something? What if they want your treatment to start as soon as possible to give you a better chance? You need to ring them.'

'Come here.' Nathan pulled Emma down onto the sofa, where they would both be able to appreciate the growing warmth of the fire. There was a blanket folded over the back so he pulled that loose for them both to snuggle under. Tonight was not a night for worrying about the maybes. There were so many of them. They'd constantly chased him all his life. They'd upset the balance of this trip. But they shouldn't be given the power to stop him living. Or Emma. 'Whatever it is, it can wait. A day or two isn't going to make enough difference to worry about it.'

'How can you be so cool about it? Aren't you worried?' Emma softened as she began to nuzzle in closer to him. She was moving on autopilot, and without meaning to she was warming him up more than any fire ever would.

For the first time in Nathan's sleep-deprived stretch, tiredness was beginning to take a hold, but he had good reason to ignore it for now. 'There's a ball of fear that I've been carrying around with me for years. It's funny how fear can drive you to do weird and crazy things, but never really to the place you want to be. There's no point in worrying about the things that aren't going to change.'

'But the dream changed, and you've been worrying about that.'

'And I shouldn't have.' Talking to a grave had made Nathan see how stupidly he was behaving. 'The whole thing is a perfect example of fearing shadows that aren't there. I've made too much of my life about things that don't exist when I should have been worrying about the things that do. And I need to apologise to you for letting it affect things between us. I never should have let it get in the way of how I feel about you.' Nathan stroked Emma's hair and admired how their bodies had navigated towards each other, like they were magnets unable to resist the pull.

In their small cocoon, Nathan was able to hear her heart beating, and he was pretty sure it was in tune with his. He'd been on such a rollercoaster with his feelings about this woman. It had been like going into freefall – the rush of adrenaline making everything seem magic, followed by the knowledge he was falling and that, if it all went wrong, there was no one to save him. No one at all.

'I love you, Emma.'

He said it before he could stop himself. He didn't want to live a life without saying the words that mattered. Especially when he'd known it since their first kiss.

When Emma smiled like a Cheshire cat, Nathan was instantly glad that he'd been brave.

'I don't quite understand it, but I love you too.'

'What's to understand? Love is love, isn't it? Surely that's all we need to know.' It was probably the first time in his life that he'd meant it. Love really was love. Once it had a hold, there was no escaping it.

There was nothing else for it other than to kiss the full and gorgeous lips that were presenting themselves so perfectly. Inviting without even trying. *This.* This was what he wished he dreamed of. The anticipation. He took in every detail of Emma's beautiful face unobscured by her glasses for a change – the scattering of freckles over the bridge of her nose, her Bambi eyes, her long dark lashes. Everything that made her so perfectly Emma.

And she was drinking in the moment the same way he was – taking in his sparkling green eyes and lightly tanned skin. They gravitated closer, one millimetre at a time.

When their lips finally pressed together, they moved in sync, and it really was what dreams should be made of.

Every second of the kiss was rousing him in ways he'd been trying to ignore until now, but it was hard to know why he'd been resisting. If anything was going to happen between them, then he needed to be fully present – not lost in repetitive, endless dreams. He needed to enjoy the moment for everything it was, and he needed to make sure Emma enjoyed it as much as he did.

Releasing himself from the kisses they were becoming tangled in, Nathan had to make sure this was what she wanted. 'We don't have to do this. If at any point you want to stop, just say the word.'

'I should let you know… I haven't done this before,' Emma said, her voice trembling.

'That's okay. You're in charge. If you're not comfortable with anything, we can stop.' Nathan was nervous in a way he hadn't experienced in a long time – to the point he was almost forgetting the basics.

It was Emma who slipped a hand under the warmth of his top, the softness of her touch kicking him back into gear.

This was the woman he loved; it was only natural that he would want to make love to her. So there was a great ease in allowing his fingertips to find their way under the fluffiest jumper known to man.

It took some exploration, but soon he made contact with her skin. It was soft and warm and silky, and her torso pulled in with a deep breath, the thrill of the moment palpable.

'Are *you* sure?' Emma asked. 'Before we do anything else. Before we go any further.'

There was a moment in which they stared into one another's eyes, each of them questioning the other without the need for words. Whatever had happened in the past didn't matter. Whatever was going to happen in the future didn't matter. All that mattered was the here and now.

'We need to use protection, but I'm sure,' Nathan said. It was a pretty obvious statement in the circumstances – even more so given his fears. But he had to let go of that. It was a dream. It wasn't based on reality. He was twenty-seven and he wasn't dead yet.

'I'm sure too.' Emma's wide eyes took him in, and her newfound confidence turned him on in ways he hadn't expected.

In fact, in every way, that's how he'd describe Emma: wonderfully unexpected.

Whatever questions he'd had before were forgotten as they relieved each other of too many layers. He drank in Emma's naked body, and even though there was an urgency within both of their speeding heart rates, he wasn't going to rush anything. He planned to savour every single moment.

Chapter Thirty-Nine

Day Twenty-Nine

Emma

There had still been a warm glow flushing through Emma's veins when she was woken by Nathan's phone chirping a Smashing Pumpkins song as way of an alarm. After a few presses of the snooze button, they'd gotten distracted with enjoying each other and ended up fast asleep again. It was probably the first time Emma had ever surfaced from bed in the afternoon. She'd made a cup of tea and then spent a good portion of time wondering how forceful she should be in trying to wake Nathan. She'd gone into pinching-earlobes mode by the time he started to show signs of life. She'd never been more relieved to hear someone groaning in their sleep. He'd barely made a peep when he'd been in his coma. And there was greater relief still when he woke, and they discussed their plans for the rest of the day. With the delay of all their snoozing, it meant they were venturing out far later than they'd planned. They wrapped up in several layers and were glad of it when they left the cottage and were met by biting winds.

'Have you replied to the hospital yet?' Despite what had happened, Emma was conscious that there were pressing matters they wouldn't be able to ignore forever.

'No, and we shouldn't let it ruin our enjoyment of today. I'm going to turn my phone off so we don't get disturbed.'

'Don't do that.' Emma was already uncomfortable about him putting off going home, but he'd managed to convince her to finish what they'd started.

'If it reassures you, I'll leave it on. I don't want to put a damper on things, but I just need to warn you that we might not see any puffins at all. We're slightly out of season for the best time of year to see them,' said Nathan, pulling her close to him as they wandered along the road.

'You mean we're putting your life at risk and we only have a slim chance of seeing what we're hoping to see?'

'You never know, luck might be on our side. The tides certainly seem to be changing on that front,' Nathan said, a twinkle in his eye as he hugged her closer.

It was cold – definitely snuggling weather. The thought of last night's antics sent a tingle down Emma's spine. She wasn't sure what she'd expected her first time to be like, but with Nathan it had been so much more than she'd ever hoped for. She'd always had her head in novels, taken by the romantic thought of saving herself for '*the one*'. Last night she'd known she'd really found him. It had been worth waiting all of those years for the right person. Completely and utterly worth it.

'I hope you're right,' Emma said. It would be a shame to come all this way for the odds to go against them. They had enough battles to win without losing this one. 'Do you believe in luck?'

'I believe that sometimes you have to make your own luck. That if you want something bad enough, you do everything you can to strive for it.'

'Does that mean you're going to jump in and go and swim to the puffins?'

'If that's what it takes.' Nathan shrugged his shoulders, as if such a thing would be par for the course. 'Or come back when there's more of them. I figure making your own luck should also involve not giving yourself a healthy dose of pneumonia in the process.'

They were nowhere near any houses now, wandering along the long, winding road that took them along the clifftop.

Emma was glad she had opted to wear a hat. Her hair would have been whipping about everywhere if she hadn't. The strong breeze was pushing them along at quite a pace, and now the only way to be heard would be to shout over the gusts of wind they were fighting against. Emma linked her arm tightly with Nathan's to make sure she didn't get blown away.

They continued down a long stretch of cliff path on their quest to the viewing points where they hoped to catch sight of the beautiful birds. Even though the wind was strong, it was possible to hear the call of seagulls carried across from the cliffs.

The North Sea stretched out to the horizon. It was a grey day, but with an edge of spring. Now and then, rays of sun burst stubbornly through the thick clouds to prove the next season was on its way. There was hope within that newness: the world going through its cycle of life. Last year's brown and yellow leaves were now crushed into the soil, ready to feed and nourish another lot of growth. That was how Emma wished she could see the chemotherapy working:

getting rid of the unwanted and allowing new growth to occur. But in reality, she knew it didn't have those romantic edges. The worst was yet to come. Along with the surgery she needed, it would be some weeks yet before she made it through her winter.

Emma paused to take in the view along the winding path towards the craggy grey cliffs letting Nathan get ahead. There were bushes and grassland all around, the green landscape dotted with purples, whites and yellows as flowers tried to make themselves known across the canvas. The wind made their petals dance against the grey, clouded backdrop. These moving bursts of colour made Emma hopeful that they'd see some puffins with the same colour contrast in their bills so she pushed on with the walk and caught up.

It was a relief to finally get to the RSPB Bempton Cliffs reserve. Taking a deep breath, Emma was glad for an excuse to rest her weary legs a while. She didn't like to think that she was in any way unfit (not that she exercised as much as she should), but with all the additional pressures her body was under, the walk had been enough to tire her out.

'Will they be able to help us? They'll know in the centre if there's been any sightings today, surely?' Emma was hopeful.

'Fingers crossed. Let's go ask.'

In the foyer there was a large puffin statue, and they posed to take a ridiculous selfie with it. The first picture to ever exist of the two of them together – and in this new social media world, taking a photo together was a big move. Some might say monumental.

'Are there any real ones about today, mate?' Nathan spoke to the helper like they were friends from way back. It would've had to have been way back, seeing as the guy behind the counter was close to the eighty mark.

'Let me show you the best places to look.'

Emma browsed the shop as Nathan was shown the areas they should head to on the map. There were all sorts of trinkets and gifts they were able to purchase. An ornamental puffin was already winking at her, wanting to come home and take residence on her bookshelf.

'This way. We haven't got long before it's too dark to see them.'

Emma took Nathan's proffered hand. Back outside, the light had already begun to change, the grey in the clouds signalling how they were shifting closer to the end of the day, the night sky already trying to form. They really had been late getting up and going, although all with good reason. The thought sent a warm glow through her body.

'The volunteer chap said down this way we're likely to see some. There's a nesting couple, so hopefully one of them might be in their usual spot. He said it was a bit further to walk, but if we hurried we'd be in with a chance of seeing them.'

The path forked off in two directions and Nathan chose the one on the right. Emma followed as they quickstepped along the pathway towards the clifftop.

The area was an impressive expanse of land, obviously protected for all the blossoming flora it had on offer. Even without being close, Emma was able to see some of the alcoves of the cliffs further away where birds were nesting and making good for the summer. Their low-toned caws echoed as if they were all in conversation together.

The walk along the coastal path was blustery and there were viewing points they could have stopped at along the way, but

Nathan was clearly on a mission. The other birds were beautiful, most of them gannets and herring gulls, but they were not what they were here to see.

Emma was slowing down, her mind and body tiring. Every day at the moment was a surprise, and at some point, her body was bound to go into shock. She just hoped it didn't end up being on a clifftop where the wind was so strong it might blow her off.

'Are you okay?' Nathan asked, realising Emma was lagging behind.

'Just tired. It's been a long couple of days.' It had been a long few weeks. And it had been quite the hike. The amount of distance they'd had to cover was deceptive, the coastline stretching out for miles.

'Come here.' Nathan turned round and lowered himself.

At first Emma wasn't sure what he meant.

'Grab my neck.'

'Why?'

'Just do it, would you?'

Emma was too fatigued by this point to argue. As she placed her arms around his neck, he secured her legs around his waist, pulling her up into a piggyback.

'We've not got much further to go.'

'You'd better hope so, seeing as you're carrying me.'

The motion of being carried was really rather rhythmic and lovely. Emma closed her eyes and rested her head on Nathan's back and shoulders. 'Thank you. Even if we don't see puffins, this has been amazing.'

Opening her eyes, she admired the view of the cliff face across the alcove and took in the wonder of being here. From her vantage point, it was hard to tell one dot of a bird from another, but there were no flashes of orange and yellow contrasting against distinctive black and white. Without the use of binoculars, the cliffs were too far away to study all of the birds nestled on its side.

'Right.' Nathan settled Emma back down onto the ground. 'The best thing to do is lie on our fronts and watch.'

Nathan took the binoculars from round his neck and crawled forward like he was in the army.

The sky was growing darker now, the clouds masking any hint of blue that had been trying to break through. It was rather ominous given that they'd not been prepared enough to bring waterproof coats.

For a moment, as Emma watched what Nathan was up to, she imagined the worst. She imagined part of the cliff side collapsing under the weight of their two bodies and the pair of them plummeting to their demise.

'Are we supposed to lean over the edge like that?' The question popped out of her mouth before she could worry about what a bore it made her sound. It was like there was a health and safety advisor parked in her head, ready to chip in about any given scenario.

'The volunteer guy said to. He said this was the best way for us to get a peek.'

Emma didn't want to question the fact the guy hadn't looked able to get into a position anywhere like this and that maybe he'd told them just for a laugh. It would be one way to get rid of tourists without having to intervene too heavily. It was so deserted, and the wind was so blustery, it wasn't exactly like anyone would hear them scream.

Emma was doing it again. She was letting her thoughts rule her actions when she should have been lying next to Nathan already.

Not waiting for another health and safety warning to reach her consciousness, Emma crawled down onto the ground and moved so she was level with him, but not so far that she might fall off the cliff.

The grass was coarse against her skin, and although it wasn't wet, its coolness was making her several degrees colder than she had been before.

'Do you want to have a look? I'm just going to check.' Nathan passed the binoculars to Emma.

Through the lenses, it was easier to get a look at the opposite cliff face. All along this coastline, the jagged cliff faces ducked in and out, creating alcoves designed by nature. It was obvious why the birds nested here, using the curves of the cliffs to find shelter from the strong winds.

Emma used the binoculars to have a closer look at some of the nests on the opposite side. None of them contained puffins, as far as she was able to see, but it was fascinating to watch how the birds were managing to cling to the face of the cliff, withstanding the elements. It seemed like an impossible feat, and yet there they were, giving a big old middle finger to the wind and the way it tried to rile them.

She was admiring another nest when Nathan's arm brushed against her as he nudged further forward. Pulling herself away from the bird vs wind spectacle, Emma moved the binoculars away to see what Nathan was up to. He now had his head and shoulders over the side of the cliff.

'What are you doing?' She wasn't exactly in the best place to try and hold onto him if he were to fall.

'Shh!' Nathan put a finger to his lips briefly and then beckoned her over.

Putting her head over the side of a cliff wouldn't be her wisest move, but being sensible hadn't exactly got her very far in life. Emma shrugged and started moving forward.

Nathan put a finger to his lips again and then pointed down.

Slowly, Emma edged towards the brink of the cliff, until she was able to see over the edge. It was the most precarious position she'd ever found herself in. She wasn't one for heights – that was one of the reasons she wasn't keen on ever doing a skydive – but it was worth being up high if it meant she'd get to see the elusive puffin. The emblem of her childhood; a symbol of her daydreams.

And there it was.

It was easy to spot once she'd slid herself far enough forward. There was just one, about three metres below them. It was puffed out and nestled neatly in its nest, its black back on display.

As if it knew it was being watched, the puffin turned its head to see who was peering over. Even without the use of binoculars, Emma was able to see the curious colour of the bird's eyes… They were dark, almost black, and rimmed with orange. It was like they were designed to make the bird stand out. As if that wasn't enough, there were the striations on its beak, majestic now it was nearing breeding season. The black, orange and yellow stripes were such a contrast to the grey cliff side and the bird's black-and-white markings. The puffin in real life was so much more than the logo she'd grown up with and the pictures she'd seen. It regarded Emma with the same level of curiosity it was receiving, and for a moment, they each examined the other's appearance like they were the strangest creatures on the earth. She remained there, taking in the sight of this gorgeous, curious bird. It made her feel earthy and whole, like somehow she'd arrived at a point where she should be. A goal achieved. It was as if staring at this puffin that she'd longed her whole life to see was giving her the renewed strength she would need. The strength to recover from cancer. The strength to survive.

'Wow,' Emma managed to whisper, not quite able to voice her thoughts.

'Cool, huh?' Nathan still had his neck out, staring in the same direction she was. 'Can I borrow the binoculars for a bit?'

Their presence didn't seem to be disturbing the puffin. The bird must be used to curious onlookers.

Carefully, Emma removed the binoculars from round her neck, making sure they weren't going to dive downwards as she passed them over to Nathan.

The nest was so close that she hadn't even thought to look through the binoculars. But as the puffin seemed happy about their presence, she would have a go after Nathan, getting a closer look at its unique beak and eyes. It was the only sea parrot about, and it was an honour to be up this close and experience it in its own environment. Emma knew she was truly blessed. She had achieved her everlasting act.

Nathan passed the binoculars back to Emma as carefully as she had handed them to him. As she peered through them, it was like the bird was playing up to the moment, enjoying the fact it was being watched. In this quiet corner of Yorkshire, it was embracing its celebrity status, posing as if to make sure she was observing its best side.

A ringing sound disturbed their bubble of mutual admiration.

'Sorry. I knew I should have switched it off.' Nathan shuffled himself back a bit so he was able to sit up and take the call.

Only he didn't.

He silenced the call and went to put the phone back in his pocket.

'If that's the hospital, you need to take it.' Emma took a last glance at her puffin and shuffled back to safety.

'It was a different number. It doesn't matter until we go back anyway.'

Nathan was impossible at times. She wasn't sure how to make him realise that knowing was important. If they were trying to contact him, it wouldn't be without good reason.

'You know I love you, don't you?'

Nathan nodded. 'And I you.'

'Can you just make sure you do everything you can to look after yourself? I've only just found you. I'm not ready to lose you yet.' It was true. Everything was just beginning. It was too early to believe it might end – though with any luck it wouldn't. With any luck, his dream really was just a dream.

'I don't want to lose you either. But I don't want to fight a battle that I'm never going to win.'

'What do you mean?' Emma had an inkling, but she needed to be sure.

'I'm not sure I want to know about treatment plans if I've got no hope of it actually working.'

'But you don't know that.' Emma was failing to keep quiet. She was also failing at keeping her cool.

Nathan's phone rang again, as if emphasising the importance of the call.

It was a huge temptation to take if off him and field the call herself. At least that way they'd know what was going on. Instead, she pleaded with her eyes like a helpless puppy. It was a pointless move, Emma realised. Whatever Nathan wanted to do, Nathan was going to do. In one way it angered her – his lack of consideration over how she was feeling – but at the same time, she knew that no one should sacrifice part of themselves based on the feelings of someone else. She had a certain admiration for the kind of headstrong nature he was displaying. When anyone stopped being themselves, they lost something in the act. Perhaps that had been happening with Emma all her life. By being a giving person, she'd eventually given away parts of herself. She'd lost herself in the process. But that wasn't how it was going to be any more.

'Hello.'

She felt her heart beat in her mouth when he answered.

'Monday. That's fine.'

Those were the only words spoken in the brief conversation.

'Is everything okay? What did they say?' Anxiety was filling the space where Emma's heart had been.

'They were just booking in my next appointment. It wasn't ever anything to worry about.'

But all of Emma's worries would be concentrated on Nathan whether she wanted them to be or not. Because sometimes dreams did come true. Her night with Nathan and seeing the puffin today were proof of that. She just had to hope against hope that the only dreams that came true were the nice ones. Because in all honesty, the one dream that Nathan kept having was truly her greatest nightmare. And she didn't want it to come to fruition. Not now. Not ever.

Chapter Forty

Day Thirty-Two

Nathan

The practice of creating everlasting acts was proving to be more fulfilling than Nathan had ever imagined, and it was catching. He wanted to do it again. And he wanted to do it before Monday. Not for distraction, but for the pleasure it would bring him.

It could wait – of course it could. Everything could wait until another lifetime if you let it.

But Nathan wasn't in the habit of letting that happen. Instead, he and Emma were on the doorstep of Rudi's flat, with Tim and Leanne waiting outside as their transport. The grey block of flats where Rudi lived reminded Nathan of why he wanted to do this. Not just what they were doing today, but way beyond that. Time and time again. He would do whatever he could to get this charity going.

It was Rudi who opened the door.

'What are you doing here?' he said, his delight shining through his question.

'Told you there was a surprise,' said his dad, who'd wheeled up behind him in the corridor.

Rudi looked from the new guests at his door to his dad, confusion folding his expression.

'All set?' Nathan directed the question at Tony, Rudi's father. They'd spoken a couple of times on the phone now.

'Yep, if you are.'

'Set for what?' Rudi asked.

'You might recall telling me about something you'd really love to do,' said Nathan. Just thinking it was making him smile.

'What? What is it?'

'You're too young to go skydiving out of a plane, but you're not too young to do indoor skydiving. Reckon you'd be up for that?'

'Are you serious?' The thrill on Rudi's face was joy itself, his gaze going from Emma and Nathan to his dad.

'Of course we are,' Emma said, her grin as bright as Rudi's expression.

'And if you're both ready, our transport awaits.' Nathan gestured for them all to get going.

Rudi put his shoes on and gathered everything he needed at record-breaking speed.

'This is so cool,' Rudi declared once they were all in Tim's minibus. Tim was in the process of setting up his own business for extreme sports, and this was the first purchase towards it. Nathan had known having a best mate with a minibus would be handy, especially when it had a wheelchair platform and access at the back. Hopefully it would be comfortable, as the indoor skydiving centre was about an hour away.

'Today will be great,' Nathan said, once they were settled and on their way. 'But as I realise it's not quite the same as jumping out of a plane, I've collected enough money for you to do the real thing once you're old enough.'

The charity fundraising page that Nathan had set up had received phenomenal support thanks to the power of social media. Nathan was paying for Rudi's indoor skydiving experience, but he already knew the charity would be able to fund his outdoor experience in the future.

'I get to do two lots of skydiving?' Rudi asked, wide-eyed.

'That's the plan. Today is just a taster.' As much as he wanted to, Nathan wasn't going to make any promises about doing the next jump with him. At least he was able to be there today. Tim was going to go in with Rudi if he was too afraid to go it alone, and Nathan would keep Rudi's father company. He'd love to join him, but the wound on his side was way too fresh for even daredevil Nathan to want to fly in a wind tunnel.

'You're going to love it, mate.' Rudi's dad nudged him on his wrist, his spinal injury limiting how high he was able to raise his arm.

Once they arrived, it didn't take long for Rudi to get ready. It turned out that he didn't need the moral support of any of the adults to find the courage to take part. Leanne and Tim were busy filming the whole event so Rudi would always be able to look back on this moment, and the rest of them were watching on from the viewing platform.

For Nathan, so much of it was reminiscent of the AirFly HQ... the jumpsuits, the set-up, the anticipation in the air. But here there was no need for parachutes or planes.

The instructor waited for Rudi to step inside the large circular chamber, and as soon as he was inside he was airborne, weighed down by the instructor who guided him through his flight. First there were a couple of rotations, during which Rudi found his balance, and then a thumbs up before the instructor guided them higher.

The instructor and Rudi looked as if they were flying. Without the usual skydiving attachments, they looked like superheroes. As Nathan was always jumping out of planes, it wasn't something he had ever done himself, but it appeared to be huge fun. It was joyous seeing what a great time Rudi was having. Maybe, just maybe, thought Nathan, if he wasn't allowed to skydive any more, this was a job he could do. But thinking like that was dangerous. At the moment, he didn't want to think beyond today.

Rudi swooped round and up the tunnel again. With the high-velocity wind pressing on his features as he flew, it was hard to tell if he was absolutely terrified or having the best time of his life.

'That. Was. A-MAZE-ING!'

If Nathan had been in any doubt, Rudi's declaration as he came out clarified how he felt about the whole thing. As with Carole's jump, everyone felt the high. It made Nathan feel warm inside in a way he hadn't experienced before these past few weeks. These weeks had been the scariest of his life and yet they had made him feel alive – reminding him what was important.

Once Rudi had hugged his dad and thanked everyone else, he made his way to Nathan.

'When I get to jump out of a plane, can I raise more money for your charity?'

There weren't many things that got Nathan right there in the middle of his chest. But that one sentence did. All of a sudden, Nathan was in need of a tissue. The kid wasn't even a teenager, but he had the insight of someone much older. Nathan was supposed to be helping him out and already he was wanting to be generous in the other direction.

'That's why we're setting this up – so people can have unforgettable experiences. It would be a total honour if you decided to do your jump to help raise money for the Everlasting Acts charity,' Nathan said.

It wasn't until later, when he'd returned home with Emma (and there was no running away from her bedroom this time), that it finally caught up with him what a big day it must have been for Rudi. 'Rudi's never going to forget this.'

'And he'll never forget you.'

Despite what he'd spent a lifetime believing, Nathan really hoped Rudi wouldn't get the chance to forget him. Maybe there was some fight in him after all.

Chapter Forty-One

Day Thirty-Four

Nathan had never done jury service.

He'd never ordered from every section of the menu.

He'd never worn odd socks, either by accident or on purpose.

He'd never managed to get covered from head to toe in mud.

He'd never eaten an entire block of cheese in one sitting.

For all he'd tried to live life to the full, it was amazing how quickly the things he hadn't done were leaping into his head while he sat in the waiting room. With every passing minute he was adding more to the list. He had to hope someone called him in soon, before the list was his very own epidemic. Once he'd started to think of things he hadn't done, he couldn't stop, and dozens of other missed opportunities began to pile up.

'Are you okay?' Emma asked from beside him.

He wasn't. But how did you answer that question without making the other person worry even more?

'I just wish they'd hurry up.' That much was true. He didn't want to be left any longer with the list that was growing in his head. Emma placed a hand on his knee for reassurance and he took hold of it like it might anchor him. There was a huge part of him that wanted to run away and not even bother with finding out what this appointment had to reveal. It was only Emma who was grounding him.

'Mr Foxdale, would you like to come through?' Nathan's specialist nurse asked him.

It was weird hearing himself being referred to as a mister. It seemed far too grown-up – he wasn't ready to be a responsible person. That was something people reserved for their thirties. But as he wasn't expecting to make it there, perhaps the time had come already.

'Do you want me to wait here? Or come in with you?' Emma asked.

Nathan wanted her with him. There was no doubt about that. The whole of life seemed easier when she was nearby. 'Come with me,' he said. 'It might make more sense to you.' Emma was definitely the brighter out of the two of them. If there was jargon he didn't understand, she would know what they were on about. And, really, he wanted her to hold his hand.

He was never going to say it out loud, but he was scared in ways he hadn't known before. Because despite thinking that he already knew what he was going to hear, it didn't make it any easier.

When they went into the consulting room, it felt like there was an army of medical staff in there, waiting for their patient. Along with the specialist nurse, Miranda, there were Dr Howson, two other doctors and two trainees. They all introduced themselves but Nathan was too busy counting the number of people to take notice of names.

'Thank you for coming in today,' Dr Howson said, like they'd popped over for a cuppa and a chat. 'Are you okay for the medical students to observe the appointment?'

'Can I ask them a question?'

The medical team all glanced at each other, as if they'd never been asked anything before.

'You mean a medical question? They are still learning, remember.'

'And maybe this will help.'

'Okay, well, if the medical students are happy to answer then I don't see why not.'

Nathan wasn't sure why he was doing this. But if he was right about what was coming, he wanted it to be done in the right way.

The two medical students were looking at him reluctantly. 'I was thinking a lot, out in the waiting room. You probably all know my medical history. You probably know that I work as a tandem skydiving instructor.' The students – a man and a woman – nodded in the right places. 'I've been sitting out there thinking about all the things I've never done. Stupid things, like I've never fallen over because of someone tying my shoelaces together or grown my own sunflower from a seed.'

Nathan wasn't completely sure where he was going with this other than to impress upon them what a human experience this was. That he wasn't just a nameless, faceless patient. That the words the doctor would provide mattered. That the sentences these students would provide in the future would stay with each of their patients for a long time, perhaps forever.

'So my question is, what's my name? And I don't mean Mr Foxdale. Hands up if you know my first name.'

The students looked at each other, perhaps hoping the answer would come if they conferred. After breaking their brief glance, the female student put her hand up.

'I've never planted a sunflower seed either, by the way. Your name is Nathan.'

To Nathan's surprise, hearing his name put a lump in his throat. All at once it was real and he was a mess. 'Thank you,' he managed to croak out.

'We should thank you,' said Dr Howson. 'It's an important lesson for all of us to remember. We shouldn't neglect the most basic patient care. And I must apologise for calling you Mr Foxdale when you would prefer me to use your first name.' The doctor moved a box of tissues closer to Nathan. 'Are you happy for the students to stay?'

Nathan grabbed a tissue, surprised to find he was already in need of one. He nodded, not able to form a sentence at that moment. He'd never intended to kick them out; he just wanted them to know this wasn't about clinical notes or diagnoses. Their future jobs would involve making a thousand differences, but they needed to never lose sight of the fact that each of those differences belonged to an individual with a name. An individual with a life span that might mean they never get round to completing half the things they wanted to.

'Thank you for letting them stay.'

Nathan nodded, not a fraction closer to feeling ready for what was to come.

'There is no easy way of saying this, Nathan… We have the results from the lumpectomy and I'm afraid it wasn't the news we were hoping for.'

The tears were steadily streaming now. Nathan hadn't expected to react like this. After so many years, he thought he'd be stoic. Instead, he was finding that there was no number of dreams that would have prepared him for this moment. 'What is the news?'

The doctor focused on the notes rather than him for a moment and took a breath before talking again. 'The lump we removed was cancerous, and I'm sorry to report it was metastatic.'

And there was the blow.

The news that winded him completely.

'What does metastatic mean?' Emma asked from beside him.

'The lump was a symptom of a secondary cancer, so that means it's already spread.'

'Oh. Shit.' It wasn't often that Emma swore, and it was the clearest indicator that this was bad news.

The news he'd been waiting for.

It meant he would never take his kids on the school run.

He would never even know if there were any kids to take on the school run.

And with every thought that came, the air in the room disappeared.

He couldn't catch his breath. He couldn't find the oxygen to keep him alive.

The pain started to trail up to his heart and the room started to swim.

'Breathe, Nathan,' Emma reminded him, grabbing his hand.

If only he remembered how.

'Don't faint on me now.'

'Nathan,' Dr Howson repeated. 'Take some deep breaths.'

His body propelled him into taking a proper inhalation. One that pushed out his ribcage rather than staying stuck in his throat.

'That's it. A few more like that,' Emma said.

He took another while his body remembered what it was supposed to do.

'Can I get you some water, Nathan?' the male student asked.

Nathan nodded, glad the student had stayed when he was offering such practical solutions. When the plastic cup was delivered, Nathan managed to steady his breath with each sip he took. The last thing he needed was another panic attack showing up and taking hold. Emma was rubbing his back and the rhythm of that was also helping.

'I'm okay. You can carry on.' However scared Nathan was, he needed to hear this. He needed to know what he was facing.

'Are you sure?'

Nathan nodded.

'Currently, it's our priority to locate the primary source of the cancer and see what treatment we can offer you.'

'What, so you don't know from the results?' Nathan was getting nervous about answers he didn't yet have. He thought cancer was good at leaving breadcrumbs, showing off about what it had been up to.

'We have an idea, but we obviously need to get full confirmation. We have you booked in for a full-body scan for as soon as possible so we can try and get some definite answers and check there isn't anything else we're missing. Are there any other health concerns you've had? Anything we need to know about? Anything your partner can think of?'

Nathan shook his head, as much in shock as to confirm that no, there wasn't anything else. Apart from… Maybe there was?

'There is one thing.' Nathan looked to Emma as he quietly said it, unsure what anyone would make of it.

'Yes?' The doctor peered up from his notes, hopeful of something that would help him.

'I've always had the same dream. I've always dreamed about dying at twenty-seven.'

It was weird to be saying it out loud, not least because it was about time he told someone in the medical profession. The weird thing was trying to describe it. Dreams weren't meant to be about dying. Dreams were meant to be about aspirations.

'Make sure we get an MRI of the brain. We need the results as a priority,' the doctor said to his registrar. 'Anything else? Any other dreams?'

Nathan wasn't about to tell him about the crying baby. The doctor would be calling a psychologist as well as ordering extra tests.

'Nope, no other dreams.' At least not ones he would achieve in his lifetime. They seemed to have disappeared along with the oxygen in the room.

Nathan's Diary

Labels are important. Or at least they can be. They seem to be in the medical world. It's like without the label they don't know how to effectively make an action plan for life.

They are on the hunt for my primary tumour. In the meantime, there are parts of me they are unable to pinpoint. Is the dream just a dream? Or is it a symptom? Is it a sign of what's wrong? They tend to discuss me, or rather it, *like I'm not present. Like I don't know what's going on. I've been admitted to the hospital. Confessing to the dream was a move too far. Now they talk to me like I've lost all my senses.*

I've argued with them. They did a scan of my head before – the unexplained coma saw to that. If there was a tumour causing my problems, surely they would have spotted it then, but apparently it wasn't detailed enough. That's why this other scan was necessary. Because they need to pinpoint me with a label. They can't have a man with mets without finding a primary. And they can't have a man with a recurring dream without finding out if the two are related.

They're not doing a very good job of hiding the lines they are drawing between the two. The recurring dreams are as a result of a tumour – that's how the thought process is going.

Is it possible the thing trying to kill me has been giving out the warning all along? And all I've done is carry on dreaming.

Chapter Forty-Two

Day Thirty-Six

The ritual of making dinner was a comforting one and Emma was opting to cook for her mother rather than the carer providing a microwave meal. Perhaps it was because Emma didn't have to think about what she was doing. She was chucking in ingredients without having to think about what went into the carbonara sauce because she already knew. The recipe was so familiar it didn't take thought or effort.

The past few weeks, it was as if someone had jammed the accelerator pedal down on her life and they weren't going to take their foot off anytime soon. It was hard to keep up. It was almost like she'd wished it upon herself, with the amount of times she'd been here cooking for her mother, feeling like she was trapped and wishing for something more exciting to come along. And now that had happened, she was half wishing she could go back to how it was before.

Only she didn't really want that. She didn't want a life without Nathan – never being kissed, never truly living. The forward acceleration might be happening so quickly that she was experiencing whiplash, but she didn't want to go back. The only problem was that what they faced ahead made the world a scary and treacherous place.

'How did it go? Is Nathan not joining us? You two seem to be getting on very well.' Carole asked once Emma was setting her up to eat at the table.

Ever since they'd returned from their trip, Carole had been asking rather leading questions, wanting more gossip than Emma was willing to give her own mother. 'It's been really nice having him stay here,' Emma said, not wanting to say more.

It only took a second for Emma's cheeks to blush furiously. The good thing about having Nathan to stay was that the magic of their trip had never really ended. Each night, Nathan stayed with her in her room. Each night, she felt like she needed to pinch herself.

'You don't need to say any more. I'm just glad to see you happy. Nathan seems like a really lovely guy and that makes me happy too. Where is he tonight?'

The other thing about carrying on with the mundane tasks of life – the bits needed in order to survive – was that it was all part of carrying on regardless. If she kept putting one foot in front of the other, she didn't have to admit to what was actually happening.

But she did.

Because without even opening her mouth, there were tears pushing through whatever persona it was she'd been trying to maintain. Autopilot was only ever going to get her so far.

'What's the matter, darling? Was it awful? Whatever it is, we'll get it sorted.' A shaky limb was offered to Emma for comfort.

'Nothing like that.' Emma shook her head vigorously. She didn't want her to get the wrong end of the stick. But she wasn't able to say why without sobbing a bit more.

'What then, lovely? Whatever it is, you can tell me.'

It was hard to breathe. It was hard to find the kind of air she needed to match the words she needed to say. Because how was it possible to say the words she didn't want to admit to? They'd not even been said by any of the medical professionals. But they'd been there in that room. Hanging in the air. They'd been there on every one of the medical professionals' faces.

Emma's mother held her, their dinner getting cold.

It was so hard to want to be anywhere but in that space. Now she was there, she didn't want to move. Who would want to gravitate away from a hug that said it would all be okay? It was a bubble that provided temporary sanctuary from the exhaustion and heartbreak of real life.

There was no escape from it though. Nathan had told her repeatedly, from early on, what he'd expected would happen. But that didn't for a second take away from the hurt she was feeling right now.

'Nathan's going to die.' Saying it out loud didn't make it any easier.

'What? What do you mean? Is he unwell again? I thought the surgery was all he needed.'

Emma had previously told her mother it was a lump and they hoped it was a type of skin cancer. It was what she had thought and hoped too. How was it sometimes the smallest things ended up being the most terrifying?

'The lump is a spread of his cancer. They don't even know where it's spread from. They have to find the main cause. They've kept him in to investigate.' With that sentence having streaked out of her, there wasn't anything left. If her mum had more questions, she wouldn't be able to answer them.

Even without knowing the source of the metastasis, Emma knew whatever news lay before them wasn't going to be good. She knew it in her gut. There was no happy ending to their story. They'd known it all along.

'There might still be things they can do. It might not be as bad as you think.'

Emma rested her head on her mother's knee while her mum smoothed her hair. It was like being a little girl again, only not. There was no amount of stroking her head that would make the pain go away.

And because the bubble was one that was so easily pierced, every inch of reality came crawling in and overwhelmed her. Every sob came so fast she wasn't able to recover from the last. She was barely able to breathe with the knowledge of how unfair her life was. If her own battle wasn't enough to face, now she'd managed to fall in love with a man who may only have months to live.

Then there was no air. The more she tried to draw it in, the less there was. The bubble was out of oxygen and she had to move or she'd be the one dying.

Emma headed for the back door and took a lungful of air like it was her first – the most important one, the one essential for survival.

The cold air hit her insides like sharp shards of ice. None of this was news. It wasn't a bolt from the blue. And yet it was, and it hurt and it was unreasonable and unforgiving, and every part of her burned with the knowledge.

She tried to harvest a sense of calm from the atmosphere and focus only on one breath in and one breath out. Then all at once, without warning, her stomach purged its contents, which landed on the grass.

She still didn't feel better. Still it was hard to breathe. However many days she had left in this life, she wasn't sure they would ever be enough to get her through the pain she was feeling right at that moment.

There would never be enough days to make this better.

Nathan's Diary

What scares a person can be revealing. There is only one thing that has ever scared me, and that is being alone.

That's quite strange considering I've spent a lot of my adult life alone. My grandparents passed within a couple of weeks of each other. My grandfather first and then – of a broken heart, it was said – my grandmother. I was eighteen and interpreted it (and the inheritance) as a sign to take on the world. To travel round it and do everything possible this life was offering me. I have kayaked through rapids in New Zealand. I have trekked to temples in India. I have thrown myself out of planes on repeat. But all of it was alone. I made acquaintances along the way, but I was on my own.

That's one thing this dream has gifted me: fearlessness. I have no fear of the usual things that people come out in a cold sweat over. The dark, heights, flying, spiders, snakes… I'm down with all of them. I'd go ahead and arrange a party involving all five.

But the dream has also gifted me my own fear – the fear of being alone. Not in the way in which some people can't exist unless they're part of a couple, but of being alone when it happens – when my time on earth is done. It makes me happy to think that, at this portion of my life, I have found good people to be around me. The concern is somehow less pressing when you know you are loved.

I've always thought that was it. That this was my only fear. That when I pass will be the time at which I will face my fear.

And yet here it is in a different form – one I hadn't expected to worry me.

An MRI scan.

It sounds simple enough. They'll take an image of my entire body. The scan will determine which parts of me are diseased. It will paint the picture of how thick a web the cancer has woven.

In the dream, I'm not alone, and that provides me with reassurance. The thought of someone not being there is what scares me.

I guess it is a rare thing to be truly alone in the world. It's not often we are left with no one to call on, though of course there are those times when we might not wish to. But I have people who'll be there for me. I know I do.

Perhaps it's time I let those people know what's going on. Tell my friends how poorly I really am.

But that won't help me with my new fear. No one is allowed in with me for the scan. They'll be no hand to hold. Just me, staying still, for as long as it takes.

It's about as alone as it gets.

Chapter Forty-Three

Day Thirty-Seven

Nathan

The noise was chugging away and the earplugs Nathan had been given weren't doing much to protect his eardrums from the sound. Its consistency was making him feel sick. Like he was on a ship and the ebb and the flow of the waves was going to set him off.

'Everything okay?' The radiographer was talking to him through the speaker.

It was far from okay. He was here being investigated for a disease that should belong to a much older man, and he was colder than he'd ever been in his life.

'I'm only twenty-seven you know.' He said it like it was what she'd been expecting to hear.

'I guess you didn't expect to be here,' said the radiographer. There was sadness in her voice. Maybe she was able to see some of the results on the screen already.

'On the contrary, I really did. That's probably the reason they're scanning me so thoroughly.'

'Okay, well, if you're comfortable, I'm going to make a start.'

The idea that it was only just starting – when he thought it had begun already – made Nathan feel nauseous all over again. 'Let's get it over and done with.'

'Just press the buzzer if you have any problems, and I can hear you if you need to talk to me.'

'Grand.'

It was so not grand. It was like the waiting room all over again, only worse. Another opportunity to fill his head with all the things he hadn't managed in his lifetime. He'd already made that list long enough… He didn't want to add to it any more.

Instead he thought about his time with Emma. About how her bedroom smelled of sweet perfume and the coconut shampoo she used. About how when they cuddled she would nuzzle into him before settling. About how they'd made love quietly and slowly and perfectly in her bed. For a while, they'd managed to exist in a time and a space outside of the hospital. It was weird to think this was where they'd first met. Where they'd spent more time together than anyone would ever care to. He didn't want to think about whether it was where they would say their goodbyes.

He needed to think about something nicer – like the puffin, and Emma's expression when she saw it. He needed to think about how that single puffin, waiting for its mate to return, was defying odds to be there. It was too early in the season. It was ignoring the weather conditions to somehow be on the edge of the cliff, like it owned the place. It wasn't going to let something like a bit of wind get in its way. Maybe that was the attitude he should take. Maybe, once they knew exactly what was going on, he should let them throw everything at him to see if he would come out alive. Would he end up defying the odds to be somewhere he shouldn't? What if he stopped believing the dream and started to imagine what twenty-eight looked like? Would it be worth putting himself through it for even the slimmest chance he would get to spend more time with Emma?

If it wasn't for the fact Nathan had been told not to move, he would kick himself. How was it that all his thoughts came around to the same thing? He was supposed to be thinking about a cute puffin. He was supposed to be thinking about the way it had made Emma smile.

Puffins. Puffins, puffins, puffins. He would daydream about them even if it was a bit nuts.

'Is everything okay in there?' the radiographer said over the speaker system.

'Yes. Just trying to think about puffins, rather than... Well, puffins are just a nicer thing to think about.' Nathan was going to explain in further detail, but it would only bring him back to the problem of not wanting to focus on that topic. So, puffins.

'I'm not sure if you realise, but you were talking out loud. I need your mouth not to be moving for the scan. Are you okay to keep still for the next part?'

Had he really been talking out loud? 'Sure,' Nathan said, pretty certain he hadn't been moving, as per the instructions.

Puffins. Puffins are cute. Puffins are fluffy. Emma loves puffins. He kept thinking it on repeat.

He repeated the phrases in his head so they matched the rhythm of the machine. It was a sweet lullaby pulling him towards sleep.

And then, there he was again.

In a hospital room…

Struggling to breathe…

Only this wasn't the room from his dreams.

There was no baby crying.

This was a theatre.

And there was an open wound. A scalpel. Searing pain.

This time, he was awake in the middle of surgery.

Chapter Forty-Four

Emma

'What's wrong? Can I go in?'

The screams were clear from where Emma was waiting, and she instinctively knew they were Nathan's. Not that they sounded like him… They were more like what she'd expect to hear from a tortured, injured animal.

She wasn't even sure who she was talking to. There was no one around in the waiting room other than a half-interested receptionist stuck behind her desk.

Emma pushed open the double doors, ignoring the hazard signs and instructions not to go in.

'You can't go in there,' the seen-it-all-before receptionist said.

'Try and stop me!' Emma said, with greater determination than she'd ever said anything before.

In the room, there was a sense of panic and more racket than Emma was able to register all at once. There was a frantic beeping noise, like the control panel of the machine in the room had completely lost all ability to function.

That noise was barely audible under the sound of Nathan's screaming. It was high-pitched and could have been almost ethereal if it weren't for the distinct note of pain being emitted.

Emma froze to the spot. It was like she'd switched to another dimension. Nathan was being hauled out of the MRI, but not with the help of medical staff, as she might have expected. Instead he was being manhandled by some security guards as if he was there to make trouble. Like anyone would ever choose to be here and then kick off.

'Don't cut me!' Nathan shouted as he tried to fight those who were trying to detain him.

'Nobody's trying to cut you, Nathan.' It should have been one of the staff trying to comfort him, but Emma found it was her mouth the words were falling from.

'It hurts.' His eyes were those of a wild animal, unable to focus. Unable to recognise any of the things around him and know who was friend and who was foe.

'You need to go outside. We're waiting for more assistance and then he'll need sedating to finish the scan.'

There was something not right about this scenario. Nathan wouldn't normally act up in this way. It was his unseeing gaze that made her realise what the problem was.

'Don't sedate him. He's not awake.' Emma knew Nathan's normal temperament and this was nowhere near it.

'He seems lively enough to me.'

'Have you ever met him before today?' Emma was fed up. She was well and truly no longer down with this shit. 'Has he ever been your patient? Do you know anything about him?'

The radiographer looked flummoxed. It was unlikely she was paid anywhere near enough to come to work and have people flip out at her. Emma immediately felt guilty, but she wasn't going to stand aside and let them sedate Nathan again. Not after what happened last time.

'Put some music on. Play Smashing Pumpkins. You need to wake him up, not sedate him.' Surely it wasn't so hard to tell that the way Nathan was acting now wasn't because of some new psychotic state; it was because even though he was moving, he wasn't awake. An adult stuck in the middle of a night terror.

'Can I ask you to leave?' It was one of the security guys now wading in on matters.

'No. You absolutely cannot. Someone here needs to be Nathan's advocate, and seeing as no one else here seems to be doing that, I'm staying put.'

'Look, love, you can see he's kicking off. There's equipment here worth a lotta money and it's here to help a lotta people. Last thing we need is him smashing it up and causing the hospital a lot of bother. We've got everyone's best interests at heart so why don't you do us a favour and let us get on with our job? We wouldn't want to have to call the police.'

'His name is Nathan. Play some Smashing Pumpkins and he'll wake the hell up.' Emma wasn't the kind of person who usually got into arguments with security guards, but then there were a lot of things she wouldn't have done until more recently. It was amazing how brave a bit of cancer was making her.

Nathan was still writhing about while being held by the security guards. Every now and then he let out another goddamn awful wail that sent a sharp shiver down Emma's spine.

The security guard grumbled under his breath and did a bad job of trying to disguise the fact he'd sworn. From his back pocket he wrangled out a phone and before long he was looking up YouTube videos. He pressed play on a Smashing Pumpkins video. 'Now you can't say that I haven't been reasonable.'

Even if this didn't do the trick, she was going to do whatever it took to stop Nathan from being sedated. Not unless there was some kind of anaesthetist present who was able to guarantee that it wouldn't send him into a coma again. And even then she wouldn't be happy about it. 'Put it on louder,' she ordered.

It was obvious the guy was going to be very quick to give up on his token gesture of kindness.

He pressed a button a couple of times. 'That's as loud as it gets.'

Emma held her breath. She didn't know what else to do to try and wake Nathan. If this didn't work, she was all out of ideas.

Fortunately it was the same song Nathan had for his alarm. Thank goodness for YouTube algorithms that knew which tunes were the most popular.

Almost as quickly as the tune had come on, Nathan focused completely on Emma. He stared into her eyes, opened his mouth and started speaking. 'I know what happens.'

Chapter Forty-Five

For all of Emma's declarations that this was out of character for Nathan, it didn't help that now he seemed to be awake, he was saying strange things.

'What?' she asked.

'I see everything.'

'Can you step away from the lady, please, sir?'

Emma didn't want him to go away. She wanted him to come back to her. She didn't know what to make of what he was saying.

'They got it all wrong.' Every statement coming from Nathan was more disjointed than the last.

The security guard took a deliberate step between them, as if Emma was under some kind of threat.

'Who got what wrong?' Emma asked, hoping she might be able to coax something a little more coherent from him.

It was hard to keep eye contact with Nathan now there was a six-foot man in her way.

'Are you going to lie down so we can finish your scan, Nathan?' The radiographer was obviously hopeful that, now he'd finished screaming and shouting, they might be able to continue. But the radiographer didn't fully understand who Nathan was, otherwise she would have known something was different. He might have woken, but it was a worry that he was now coming out with statements like he was the son of God.

'Yes, but I already know what it'll show you.' Nathan wandered back to the MRI machine and lay down like none of the last few minutes had even happened.

Emma really hoped it was a temporary glitch, like before. When he was in the coma she'd thought she'd lost him, but then he'd returned to his true technicoloured self. She didn't want to witness a gradual peeling away of his character. It was all too much as it was. She didn't want to face it without Nathan. Perhaps even Jesus Nathan she could cope with.

'Do you want us to stay?' one of the security guys who'd been restraining Nathan asked the radiographer.

'If you could hang around for a while. Just in case.'

'Just don't let him fall asleep again,' Emma pointed out, like she was selling some magic secret formula.

'You can wait outside,' the radiographer said to Emma.

'Did your mother never teach you to say please?' Emma wasn't going to be spoken to like that. She was no longer one for being a pushover. Everything was different now.

Emma was given a look from the radiographer that said: '*My mother taught me how to say fuck off.*' The temptation to say something in response was overwhelming.

But not as overwhelming as Emma's need to puke.

This time it came without warning and was unapologetic in its delivery. One heave and it was all over the security guard. Another and it splattered onto the radiologist's shoes.

'I knew that was going to happen,' Nathan said, like it was all just a comedy of errors. As life kept proving, nobody knew what was going on. Not even the people in charge.

Nathan's Diary

I do know what's going on. Or at least I now know what went on. More specifically, I remember what was being said during the surgery. I already had fragments of the procedure tucked away like scenes in a movie, but now I remember the script. 'He's bound to be riddled' is the main thing I've remembered. That and the pain of a scalpel cutting through flesh.

If I close my eyes I can feel the cold metal slicing through my skin.

For some, knowing that their time on earth is limited might be too much. Perhaps it has been for me, and it's gradually working its way out of my system. But getting the confirmation before having to wait for any kind of scan result has given me the reassurance I've needed. For too long I've wondered if the dream was me losing a grasp on reality, and now I know.

Of course, everyone is looking at me like I've gone completely nuts. Like finally I have taken leave of my senses. I'm sure the number of medical students being paraded around the end of my bedside has multiplied tenfold, like my disease is some kind of spectator sport.

I know what is going on. I've known it all along. Like I always believed, I'm going to leave this world and become forever twenty-seven.

I'm dying. But then again, aren't we all?

We're all only one everlasting act from the end.

Chapter Forty-Six

Day Forty-One

Emma was now an in-patient herself. It turned out if someone puked over enough people and got mildly violent at the same time, it wasn't going to be overlooked. They'd decided they wanted to keep her in for blood tests to make sure it wasn't anything that would prevent her from starting treatment. They didn't like anyone to have an infection or similar when they were due to have major surgery and chemotherapy commencing soon. She felt fine, though, so was escaping to Nathan's bedside whenever she got the chance. There were advantages to being admitted onto the same ward.

Today, Nathan's half-brother, Marcus, had arrived, and within two seconds of meeting him Emma had decided she didn't like him. It was when she'd gone to shake his hand and he'd very deliberately left her hanging that she realised everything that Nathan had told her was obviously true. He was taller and scrawnier than Nathan, with a different accent. They were like two sides of the same coin that didn't match up somehow.

'Can we talk to you both privately for a minute, before we speak with Nathan?' Dr Howson asked.

'Of course,' Marcus said.

Emma didn't like it. She didn't like Marcus turning up and getting to act like he was some kind of spokesperson all of a sudden, and she didn't like the fact the doctors wanted to speak to them away from Nathan. Shouldn't anything relating to Nathan's care also be shared with him as the patient? It only seemed fair. She certainly wouldn't be too happy if they were taking her mum away for a quiet word about her own condition without filling her in on what was going on. There was something not right about it.

'Shouldn't we be waiting for Nathan and discussing it when he's here?' Emma's heart was thumping. She wasn't a pushover these days and she was going to give a voice to the concerns in her head.

'We want you to be fully prepared. It's best we have a word.'

Was it? Emma didn't know what was for the best any more, but one thing was for sure: she didn't want Marcus to find out things that he might never pass on. She needed to brave listening to the doctor too, even if the thought was making her feel nauseous all over again.

She followed as the doctor led them into a side room.

'Thank you. I wanted to forewarn you both that we're going to give Nathan his full diagnosis shortly. I'm afraid the news is not good. The only options available to him are palliative. We have some ongoing concerns so the plan is to keep him in for now.'

'What does palliative mean?' Marcus asked, while Emma struggled to take in what was being said.

'It means we are dealing with end of life. Any treatment would only work to make Nathan comfortable.'

'But he's so well,' Emma found herself saying. 'We're not talking about end of life happening soon.' They couldn't be.

Before this moment, Emma had never really believed Nathan's predictions about his own death. He was the most dynamic person she knew. It didn't seem possible that his energy and spirit were going to be taken away from him. Anything but.

'Nathan has a very aggressive form of cancer that is affecting the lining of his brain. It will no doubt be part of the reason he can be so maverick. There's a chance he's been masking any pain that he's been in, but the signs that he's struggling are becoming more obvious. We don't like to talk about timescales as they can be so hard to predict, but I'm afraid we're talking days and weeks, rather than months and years.'

Emma went numb. It was hard to comprehend that something as important as how much life was left, how much time they would have together, could be delivered in such a cold and blunt manner.

But numb was good. Numb was what she needed to be. It meant she was able to leave the room and hold Nathan's hand without feeling the blow of the words as they were delivered to him as well. It meant when he sobbed on her shoulder she was able to hold him and comfort him without the need to cry herself.

She was beyond feeling. She was beyond knowing what to do. Because what did anyone do when they found out the love of their life was dying? What was anyone supposed to do when holding hands was the only thing they could manage?

Nathan's Diary

Meningioma. That's what it's called, this thing that is killing me. They say I've probably had it for years without any symptoms. They say it has effectively lain dormant, but now it has become malignant. The lining of my brain has cancer and there is nothing they can do about it because it is already too late.

It's strange, because now I know about it I think I can feel it. In all the movements I make it is there. If I stretch, it hurts. If I move too fast, it hurts. If I yawn, it hurts.

Things that weren't problematic a day ago now seem like the most impossible tasks. Putting my shoes on earlier took an extraordinary amount of effort – so much so that by the time I was done, I no longer wanted to go outside like I had planned.

This shouldn't be a shock. This is everything I predicted. Everything the dream predicted. It is a conviction I have lived my life by. And now here it is. In its fullness it is so much more than I could ever have prepared for.

Things change. My life has changed. I love Emma, and having only just met her, I'm going to have to leave her. How can that be right or fair? It's not. It won't ever be. Perhaps the shock is not in dying, but in having found someone willing to love me for exactly who I am. Even if a diagnosis is making me question exactly who that is.

The doctors are talking about the dream like it's a discussion on the chicken and the egg. There has been much debate on how the meningioma must have caused the dream and therefore has always been a symptom that I've been ill, but there are those that think the dream precipitated the growth of the cancer. Then there are those who think the meningioma has given me the gift of second sight; that it gave me the ability to predict my own death and yet not the ability to see how I would die.

If that's true, I've been given a pretty naff superpower. If I really had been given the ability to look into the future, I'd like to be more like telepathic Marvel character Charles Xavier, and do some good with my ability. But one reoccurring dream doesn't count as having true second sight. Especially when ultimately it seems to have had no purpose. All I get to do now is die. Mine is not exactly the most triumphant story of all time. I'm the kid who predicts he's going to die all his life, then he dies. The End.

And the sad truth is that I'm never going to know how it ends. I won't know if Emma gets through this. I won't know if her treatment is a success. I won't know if she'll go on to have children – our children – or if the baby I hear has anything to do with us. What will happen to her mum? Will Emma ever be happy again once I'm gone?

If this was some kind of ability, the dream would change and show me those things. Instead it lingers every night with its same stale reminder that these are my final days and that I will never have answers about what happens once I am gone. Only the certain knowledge… Twenty-seven was always my time to go.

Chapter Forty-Seven

Day Fifty-One

Emma was being kept in for longer than she'd like. Two extra weeks so far. She felt fine now. She was self-diagnosing herself with stress-induced vomiting. At the time it had happened, her heart had been so churned up with worry that it was no surprise her stomach had decided to let go of its contents. But some of her bloods had indicated raised inflammatory markers (that was how the doctor had explained it) and they were waiting for them to return to normal levels before releasing her. They were being extra cautious with her mastectomy surgery scheduled for two weeks' time, all being well.

The good thing about being an in-patient at the same time as Nathan was the fact she was able to see him whenever she wanted. And although the nursing staff kept bothering Emma about being in the men's bay, she was ignoring them quite happily.

The problem with being stuck on the ward meant there were vast amounts of time where they needed to occupy themselves. It wasn't like they were able to do fun things like share a bed, there was only so much mileage to be had from books and sudoku that were impossible to concentrate on.

Questions Emma didn't want to ask kept popping into her head. She tried to ignore them, but then there was never going to be a good time to ask. She really wished she didn't have to. She reminded herself she was being pragmatic. It was better to ask and know the answers than to keep quiet and have to guess.

'I know this is a bit morbid, but I figure I need to ask… What do you want to happen for your funeral?' The words rushed out of her. She said it really quickly in the hope that doing so would make it less hard. It didn't. She wanted to cry immediately at the thought. Every time she saw Nathan and there was a little less of his energy, she wanted to cry. But so far she'd managed not to in his presence. For him and what he was facing, she was going to keep her shit together.

'My brother can arrange all that, surely? I don't want to burden you with thinking about that when you have to concentrate on getting better.'

Emma didn't have the heart to tell him his half-brother had already gone home and didn't plan to return until Nathan was '*nearly at the end*'. They shared DNA, but that didn't mean family to some people. Marcus hated his father, and in turn seemed to hate Nathan for being related to their father. She'd been completely incensed when Marcus had said he was going, but having a brother herself who was just as useless made her realise any attempts to improve their relationship would be futile. If the only quality time Marcus could afford to spend with his brother was when he was nearly dead, well, he wasn't the kind of person Emma was about to encourage to stay for longer. Nathan deserved better.

'Would you really trust your brother with the arrangements? You need to tell me so I can make sure he does everything to your wishes, rather than his own.' It was strange to think how differently people perceived things – that one person arranging a funeral might do things in a completely different style to another. All anyone ever got to know were parts of a person, not the complete whole. Even Emma didn't know the whole map of the man she was in love with. Only he was able to fill in the blanks of what he would want, without diluted input from the cast of people in his life.

'I guess one of the major advantages of always knowing it was on the cards means I've done the prep work.' Nathan reached into his hospital side unit and produced his wallet.

'You've already made a will?' He was more organised than Emma if he had. She really needed to do the same, just in case, but then she really didn't want to believe she would be in the position of needing one anytime soon.

Nathan produced a card from his wallet and passed it over. 'This has my solicitor's details. He knows all my wishes, when the time comes. We don't need to talk about it now and upset each other.'

Emma stared at the card, unable to produce a response immediately. Nathan being prepared removed so much of the awkwardness, and yet holding this small piece of card made it even more real.

'Emma Green, I should have known I would find you in the wrong bay.' It was one of the nurses who were forever chastising her for being in the wrong place. Fortunately she was being light-hearted in her jesting or Emma might have burst into tears right there and then.

'You two have your appointment with the fertility centre soon. Are you going to walk down or would you like me to order a porter for either of you?'

'We can walk,' Nathan said. 'You'll have to bear with me, though. Everything seems to take twice as long at the moment.'

Emma tucked the card away safely in her purse. As they made their way, it was like she was taking someone else to the appointment. The Nathan who had given her a piggyback, who had organised a barbeque in the middle of winter, who had chaperoned her across the country to see puffins, was barely there. It was a painful reminder of what was occurring. One of them was dying. One of them needed to do everything possible to find the power to survive.

There was no joy to be found in their slowness. Normally, with life so often lived at breakneck speeds, she would enjoy this pace, but today it was a certain reminder of how much things had changed. Nathan's movements were visibly slower, as if his diagnosis had come along and invaded his very core.

'We need to talk about something happy. We need to decide what to call our babies when they come along,' Nathan said. There was a smile on his face that overcame everything else.

Emma was glad to be given something else to talk about, her thoughts having got stuck on maudlin matters. 'Do you know? Have you had names lined up forever?' Emma had thought about it, but she'd never come up with a concrete name. She figured it was a two-person job.

'Let's go for middle names first. That's always easier. Is it too egotistical just to call shots on Emma or Nathan as a middle name?'

'Carole needs to be one of the middle names for a girl, even if does make it bit long-winded. Then we need first names to go with them.' Emma had always liked her mother's name. She'd always wanted to honour her mother in that way.

'Juliet as well. I know I never knew my mum, but I'd like to remember her all the same.'

Nathan had never mentioned his mother's name before. 'Juliet is a beautiful name. One of my favourite Shakespeare characters. I like that as a first name.'

'That was easy. What about for a boy?'

'I like Romeo, but there's no way we're going for a matching set. What do you like?' Emma found herself smiling. That was why they were doing this – to find hope in a desolate, dark corridor where there would otherwise be none.

'I've always liked shorter names for a boy. Something like Logan or Thor.'

'Or Bruce, perhaps?' Emma was able to recognise a theme. It was a shame that, between the pair of them, they didn't have any male role models they wanted to recognise with name-giving honours.

'You got me. Do you have anything else you like?'

It was quite the conversation to be having as they reached the foyer for the lifts. They needed to go up two floors for the appointment. How much was it possible to plan in the shortest of times? Emma held the door open for Nathan, as she was ahead.

'I rather like your name. Is Nathan Junior a cool name for a kid?'

'Nathan Thor Junior is cooler.'

'Juliet Emma Carole and Nathan Thor Junior. Is that what we're going with?' The lift doors opened and they stepped inside.

'I think they're perfect,' Nathan said, as he rested an arm on the lift wall, the walk having evidently worn him out.

Emma gave him the softest kiss on the cheek as the doors closed. For a moment, while the lift travelled upwards and they were in their own little bubble, they curled into each other. Catching a moment alone together. It was precious when there were so few of these occasions to be had.

And even though it had been the slowest of journeys, it was scary how quickly decisions could be made when life was changing at a pace they'd never be able to meet.

Chapter Forty-Eight

The procedure Emma went through wasn't exactly pleasant, but as her last one had been a breast biopsy, in comparison it wasn't a big ordeal. There was some mild discomfort involved, and the awkwardness of having her legs in stirrups while they were harvesting her eggs was a joy, but it didn't take long as they counted each one they found. Despite the mild local sedative, it was one of the simpler moments she'd experienced over the past couple of months, which was saying a lot.

The worst part of it all was Nathan not being with her. He'd been whisked off to provide his own sample so that it was ready for when her eggs were harvested, following which the two samples would be fused to form one. Their potential embryos for the future. The weirdo stranger who'd become her friend.

The assumption that they were partners had led to them becoming an actual couple. It seemed so cruel that she would lose him and then have her own fight on her hands. She just hoped that what they were doing today would come to fruition. That the future might hold more hope than the present.

When she was finished, Nathan was in the waiting area. He looked grey, as if his colour had been flushed away.

'Did it go okay?' Emma hoped that encompassed: '*Did you manage to provide a sample?*' without her having to say it. She really wasn't sure how else to ask.

'It wasn't the same without you.' Nathan raised an eyebrow.

'Quite.' There were people about, but that didn't stop Emma from kissing him. It wasn't much more than a peck – a tender kiss between two people who loved each other. The connection between them was no longer questionable. Emma would have been more passionate, but it was clear Nathan was worn out.

'Shall we call you a porter for the return journey?' a nurse asked.

'I'll wheel him back, if that's okay?'

It took the nursing staff at least ten minutes to get permission and locate a chair.

'Do you think they're putting them together now? That right now our future is in a Petri dish?' Nathan said.

'I don't think they wait long. They managed to harvest eight eggs.'

'Eight? That's amazing. We might not have picked out enough names after all.'

The nurse delivered the wheelchair and Nathan struggled to stand and fold his tall frame into it.

'Will you be okay getting back?' the nurse asked.

'I'm sure they'll give you a call if we go AWOL.' Emma wasn't even joking. The nurse that had sent them was a proper taskmaster.

Emma was glad to get into the lift. The clinic was pleasant enough, but there was no taking away from the fact that it was a clinic. That they were there for a reason and it wasn't the natural course of a relationship.

'How are you feeling?' Emma asked, noticing how Nathan was sitting rather heavily in the wheelchair.

Nathan's head was resting in his hand, like he had a bad migraine he wasn't able to shift. 'Today has really taken it out of me. I think I need some sugar to revive me.'

'We can stop for a drink on the way back. Go AWOL for a short while?'

'I think I need to go and lie down. Maybe we could pick up a pack of sweets on the way back? That might help.'

Emma nodded and they carried out their short mission in silence.

Nathan obviously wasn't feeling like himself and it was clear that their short trip had exhausted him. It was like he'd given his all to make sure whatever was occurring in the Petri dishes was their absolute best shot. Their greatest hope for the future.

Once Nathan was curled up under his pale blue hospital blanket, clearly in need of sleep, with the Skittles they'd purchased unopened on the side, Emma retreated to her own bed space. It was getting harder and harder not to cry in front of Nathan with every day that passed, with every diminishment she noticed.

Today was a miracle. Today Nathan had gifted her the potential to create life. She just wished it wasn't at the expense of his energy.

Wrapped in her own hospital blanket, the curtains pulled around her bed, Emma cried the tears she couldn't bear Nathan to see.

She cried and she prayed. Because while she was the saddest that she'd ever been, she wasn't beyond hope. At the very least, today had to mean that some hope was theirs to be had.

Chapter Forty-Nine

Day Sixty-Four

Emma's days were merging into a blur. She no longer had a reference as to what day of the week it was. There were no markers to help her get her bearings. A Monday looked the same as a Thursday and it was hard to keep count of the passing hours.

Not long after their fertility appointment, Emma had been discharged. Now she rose early each day to be at the hospital as soon as visiting hours started, and she would spend her time there, only leaving for lunch when visitors weren't allowed on the ward. She would spend a lonely lunchtime trying to source some reasonably healthy food and trying not to bump into anyone she knew. Some afternoons, when visitors were allowed on the ward again, one of Nathan's friends would join her. Normally it was Leanne or Tim. Every visit was a struggle.

The struggle was mostly Nathan's. It went against his character to allow his friends to see him like this – the maverick reduced to a man who struggled to stand without help.

It was a hard thing to witness, this gradual deterioration, but Emma didn't want to be anywhere other than by Nathan's side. Even on the days like today when he was lethargic and needed to sleep.

'Emma,' a voice whispered.

Emma turned, expecting to find one of the nursing staff wanting to get to Nathan's bedside to disturb his slumber and take his observations.

'Hey, sweetie. I've brought hot chocolate.'

It was Alice. The surprise of seeing her almost made Emma burst into tears. It had been weeks since they'd last seen each other. She was so used to catching up with her best friend at least twice a week that not seeing her had felt like another punishment the cancer was dishing out.

Elated by her friend's presence, Emma got up and gave her a hug, even though it was a bit awkward with the cups still in Alice's hands.

'I hope you don't mind... I chatted to your mum and she said it should be okay for me to pop by. Also, these aren't posh hot chocolates – I made them at home. But I do have squirty cream and marshmallows in my bag to make the experience just as good.'

'It's lovely to see you.' It was funny how sometimes you didn't realise something was missing until the moment it came back. So much had happened in recent weeks, Emma wasn't keeping up with herself, let alone anyone else.

'Take this.' Alice passed Emma one of the thermos mugs. 'We need to get comfy and pretend we're in a coffee shop, putting the world to rights. Will Nathan be okay with us taking over his bed space?'

Nathan was in a deep sleep. He often slept for two to three hours in the afternoon on top of a full night's sleep.

'I don't think he'll mind. It's normally his friends here and he has to wake up for that. At least if you're here to see me he can get some extra rest.'

Within minutes, Alice had managed to arrange an extra chair and had added the cream and marshmallows to their drinks. She'd even brought along some of those wrapped caramelised biscuits to go with it. 'I need to make sure your calorie intake is up.'

Emma smiled, but her gaze was drawn to Nathan. The figure in the bed whose energy was decreasing every day. She wished an overdose of sugar would have him bouncing around the room. If only it were that easy.

'How's he doing today?' Alice asked.

Emma had been providing Alice with frequent updates by text. But there were subjects for which the words didn't exist. Even now, with him close by, it was hard to put it all into a sentence. Every day there was less of him – a microscopic shrinking. The Nathan she knew was still there, but she'd had to watch as pulling on a sock became an impossible task, while his appetite waned and she had to remind him of the tasks he should be carrying out. 'About the same.' Emma screwed up her face a little and dipped her ear towards Nathan's bed.

'I get ya,' Alice said, knowing that Emma was indicating she didn't want to say too much at his bedside.

'Thanks for this.' Emma helped herself to her first marshmallow. It was a sweet gesture, but not one that totally took away from their surroundings.

'It's good to see you. It's been strange without you about. I figured, as you couldn't get to me, I needed to come and see you. I wish hot chocolate was able to cure a whole lot of ailments, given the circumstances.'

Emma took a sip. 'At least it's providing a hug in a mug, if nothing else.' Her voice slipped, losing any note of humour she might have been going for.

'Your mum is worried about you. She thinks you should be resting at home today.'

Emma let out a long sigh. 'Did she send you?'

'No, I was coming already. I'm not here trying to negotiate for her. I'm just a bit worried she might be right. It's your surgery tomorrow. It wouldn't hurt for you to be at home, resting. Nathan would understand that.'

'I'm not leaving him.' Emma said it with the ferocity of a woman who'd been constantly justifying her position for some time.

'And I'm not leaving either,' Alice said.

'What do you mean?'

'I knew you wouldn't want to leave. And the problem is, I'm your best friend, so there isn't any occasion I should side with your mother over you. But as it stands, if you are not going to make sure you look after yourself, I'm going to make sure for you.'

Emma didn't want to be upset or frustrated with her best friend. But right now, she was tired and exhausted and she didn't want to lay out all the reasons she was beyond thinking. 'I don't need babysitting.'

'Nobody has said you do, sweetie. But if there was ever a time I should be looking out for you, I think that time is now. And I know one of the things you don't want to do is leave Nathan by himself any more than necessary. So, today, if you want to leave early, I'll be here until they kick me out. And the same tomorrow.

While you're having surgery, I'll be here keeping your seat warm until you're well enough to take up your place again. I'm not about to frogmarch you home and tell you what to do – I'm pretty certain you already know how you need to prepare – I'm just offering some gentle encouragement towards you going home a bit early and doing everything you can to be ready. A long soak in the tub and an early night are in order, if nothing else.'

Emma glanced at Nathan. There was a soft rumbling as he exhaled – not quite a snore, but a signal he was enjoying his slumber. Would it really matter if she left a few hours early?

She didn't want to, she knew that. She wanted to be by Nathan's side. But, within that, she also knew there was a reluctance for it to be her turn. Knowing what Nathan had been through over the past few weeks was easily enough to put her off. She wanted to bury her head in the sand for as long as possible.

'I just feel so guilty.' There were so many wrongs that she wished she was able to make right. Life wasn't fair. Nathan was clearly struggling and there was nothing that the doctors were able to do other than provide pain relief. It was ironic to be feeling such a wrench about going to get herself better.

'You don't need to feel guilty.' This time it was Nathan talking to her.

'How long have you been awake?' Emma had been sure he was still sleeping.

'Not long. But long enough to know that you should be taking Alice up on her offer.' Nathan made efforts to sit upright and managed to get there without help.

Emma was already waiting in the wings, ready to assist if needed.

'Look, you've been doing plenty of looking after me and your mum. For once, you need to make sure you're the priority.' Nathan tucked Emma's long hair behind her ear, their foreheads almost touching. 'Just promise me you'll pop by tomorrow morning before you go in, even if it doesn't fit in with their visiting hours.'

Emma pressed her forehead against his and took his scent in: cedar wood and salty skin. 'I promise.'

There weren't many things she was able to hold on to at the moment, but when good friends were looking out for you at least it eased the strain slightly.

What would come would come. Today was one of the rare occasions when she was able to prepare herself. Whether she was ready to was another matter entirely.

Chapter Fifty

Emma peered down at her naked form in the bath. For someone who was used to being alone, she hadn't had much time to herself in recent weeks. Whenever she'd been home, it had mostly been for the purpose of sleep, and over the past few weeks she'd preferred quick showers where she paid little attention to her body. But this was a weird occasion. Almost like a ceremonial bathing. This was the last time this would be her shape. After tomorrow, the contours of her body would be different.

It was hard to know how to feel about it. Hard to even imagine. When she did, it made her want to cry. But then she reminded herself of the reasons why this was happening. As she soaped a flannel and brushed it against her skin, the breast they were removing already felt alien, the inverted nipple a telltale sign of something wrong. She was glad, at least, that she would no longer possess that reminder of being unwell. The operation would make her healthy and put her on the road to recovery.

She would be well again.

She would find whatever it took to get herself through this.

She would wear her warrior paint with pride.

But for now, she would allow herself to cry in the bathtub.

She would cry for feeling alone.

She would cry for the injustice.

She would cry for Nathan.

She would cry for the life that would never be.

Nathan's Diary

It's happening so quickly, I don't even know how to fathom it. I barely have the strength to write it down. I think, now I know I'm dying, the process has sped up. I should fight it, I know I should. But for what purpose? For Emma to spend another heartbreaking day watching me struggle? I can't let that carry on when she needs to look after herself.

Never have I ever wanted it more – for the dream to become a reality. For it all to finally make sense.

Hospital room…

Struggling to breathe…

A baby crying…

Come to me. I am waiting.

Chapter Fifty-One

Emma

On the day of Emma's surgery, she only got to see Nathan briefly, and he was too sleepy to be woken. Alice kept her promise, keeping him company that day. She'd been too busy worrying about him to allow concerns about her own surgery to reach her until she was being wheeled into the theatre.

When it was over, Emma kept reminding herself that the main thing was that the surgery had gone well. And all things considered, she wasn't feeling too sore.

On day one, Emma ate, sat in her chair and walked for the first time, but Nathan wasn't able to visit.

On day two, Emma had her drain taken out and was allowed to try the stairs ready for discharge, but Nathan wasn't able to visit.

With the surgical and medical wards at separate ends of the hospital, they were entire worlds apart, as far as Emma was concerned.

On day three when she was due to be discharged, at last she was given permission to walk down to the other end of the hospital to see him. She'd been desperate to make this journey, to see for herself how he was doing. Texts from Nathan and updates from her mum only told her so much.

'Take your time, love,' Emma's mother said from beside her.

'I still think you should let me sit on your lap so we can get there quicker.'

'I'm still getting used to this chair. I don't think my steering will be very good if I can't see where I'm going. Besides, I think the days of you sitting on your mother's knee are long gone.'

'I should hope so too.' Emma stretched a little taller and walked more consciously than she normally would. She was aware of the arch of her spine, the pull of her muscles, the placement of her feet on the vinyl flooring. It was strange how one adjustment to her body had altered her balance.

And as she strode along the corridor with her mother beside her, it was pleasing to be able to feel this adjustment. To know that there were changes within her body that were positive in ways she was yet to fully appreciate. The thought made her stretch taller again. As if along that section of corridor she was acting out Charles Darwin's theory of evolution.

It was taking all her strength and there was a pulling sensation across her chest, but there was nothing that was going to stop her right now. No distance would prevent her from seeing Nathan. No illness would stop her from getting better. No hurdles would prevent her from getting to the finishing line, wherever that might be.

When she did get there, Nathan's ward was different. The light was more intense and everything seemed to be clearer, like when she'd worn glasses for the first time and her full vision returned.

Nathan was sitting in the ward's day room. It was unusual to see him there, making it a staged ceremony. He was thinner, his cheeks sallow. There was a blanket over his knees, as if he were an old man.

Emma had to take a moment before sitting with him. She glanced at the plastic plant and the battered magazines on the table and wondered how any of this was real. Surely this wasn't the same man she'd met in a waiting room not so long ago?

But of course it was the same man. Whatever changes were occurring, in whatever direction they were going, they would always be Nathan and Emma.

Emma took the waiting seat, leaving her mum browsing a bookshelf.

'It looks like I need to lend you my copy of *Robot Wars Monthly*,' Emma said.

'I've missed you.' Nathan smiled, before gingerly leaning forward and kissing her on the cheek. 'Any chance you feel up to smuggling me out of here?'

Emma only wished she could. This would be one of the last times they would sit together like this.

It was a sad truth that as one of them was gearing up to leave, the other never would. And it was evident how much had changed in the few days she'd been away. If she hadn't known Nathan was poorly before, it was now painfully clear.

Chapter Fifty-Two

Day Eighty-Eight

Arguing was hard at the best of times. Finding the conviction to stand up for one's beliefs required a bold approach that not everyone was capable of. And it was even harder when still recovering from surgery. The past few weeks had been the hardest Emma had ever endured and even now she didn't know if she was putting her convictions in the right camp.

'He should stay here.' It wasn't exactly an eloquent argument when faced with a team of medical professionals. Nathan's decline seemed to be more rapid than any of them had been expecting.

'The hospice is a much nicer setting and is more equipped to deal with this stage of things. I've spoken to Nathan's brother who is in agreement. We feel it is for the best and we'd like your approval. We'll prepare Nathan for the move as soon as there's a bed available.'

Of course Nathan's half-brother thought it was a good idea. He had no idea. He probably wouldn't even rush to get down here, having not witnessed how things had deteriorated so drastically.

'But he has never expressed any wish to go to a hospice. He's been happy here. I don't think the disruption will be good for him.' Emma couldn't voice the real reason she wanted him to stay at the hospital for his final hours. The doctors thought his dream was caused by his illness, and they would be unlikely see it the same way Emma did.

The real reason she didn't want him moved was because a hospice wasn't part of the dream. Even though she should be doing everything in her power to make sure the dream didn't occur, she was also aware that if the end was how he expected it to be, then somehow it would provide comfort for him. Nathan was barely lucid, but she wanted to keep whatever parts of what she knew he had believed in to be true to form. It was stupid, she realised that. It hardly made the dream psychic if she augmented life to fit in with what he'd dreamed. But surely there would be comfort in familiarity. If it happened how he'd always thought it would, wouldn't that be a less stressful way for him to go?

Heartbreakingly, Nathan was too out of it to give his opinion. When Emma said his name, he would turn his head towards her voice and flutter his eyes open briefly, but that was it. When she held his hands, his skin was rough and every part of him seemed frailer. It was only a few weeks since his diagnosis and it was terrifying how quickly he was wilting away.

Emma spent portions of time wishing she was able to make it go away. She smoothed moisturiser into his hands to make them feel less sore. She rubbed Vaseline onto his lips when they started to crack and she held his drink to his mouth when he was unable to lift it himself. Day by day he was inching further away from the place they had been. He was inching further away from life.

'It really is the best place for him. You'll be free to visit whenever you choose there.'

Emma was having to spend the nights at home, struggling to sleep. She was leaving reluctantly when visiting hours ended, not wanting to be away from Nathan's side. She didn't want him to be alone when he went. Knowing it was his biggest fear, it was important to Emma that it never happened that way. She'd vowed to ensure it didn't.

'Why don't you take the night to think about it? Maybe you'll feel differently in the morning.'

It was one way for her opinion to be shrugged off, but to be honest, she was so tired and so incapable of reasonable thought that she was no longer sure what was for the best.

Coming home to her mother had never been nicer than in the past few weeks. With her mum's care provided for it no longer felt like she was returning to work. These days it was often the case that she went home to unburden.

Carole had already been put in bed by the evening carer. There was a chance she would be asleep, but Emma slipped into the front room to check on her, as she always did. On the nights her mother was still awake, she'd fill her in on what was happening. It allowed a good old blub away from Nathan if she needed it.

'How are things?' Carole asked, before she was fully through the door.

'Not good.'

'How so?' Her mother moved in her bed so she was able to listen more intently to her daughter.

'They want to transfer him to a hospice.'

'Oh, sweetheart. They think that's necessary already?'

Emma slumped down into a chair, finding that she was way too exhausted to stay upright any longer.

'He really is just fading away. I think he said my name about three times today. That was it.'

'Do you think the move to the hospice is a good thing?'

That was the thing about mums. Sometimes it wasn't necessary to vocalise what was wrong because they'd already sussed it out.

'I don't know, Mum. This is going to sound silly, but he always said that in his dream he died in a hospital room. I know that it's all make-believe, but I can't help but think it would be more comforting if at least some elements of the dream came true.'

'But is a hospice room much different to a hospital room? Would he even know the difference?'

Emma shrugged. She'd never been to a hospice to know what their rooms were like. 'So you think I should agree? His brother already has.'

'I think, right now, you need to choose your battles. I'm not sure this is one of them.' Carole reached for her daughter's hand and Emma took hold of the gesture.

The weight of everything made her take in the biggest sigh. 'It just doesn't seem right that it's ending this way.' Despite the dream, despite everything in it, Nathan's life was being extinguished so quickly. It was impossible to think that such a bright light could be dulled in this way.

'I know what you mean, love. Nathan is something else. I can see why you've fallen for him.'

Emma well and truly had. She'd never been one for talking about destiny before. For her, destiny had only ever existed in the pages of the books that she'd read. Until Nathan. He'd bundled into her life so quickly, just when she needed him, and the unjustness of him leaving as fast was almost too much to bear. 'I'm not ready for him to go.' A sob made her pause. 'Not yet.'

'I don't think we can ever prepare ourselves for these things. Especially with someone so young and with so much life. But we have to look to the positive. Wherever possible, you and I need to look for the positive.'

'What can possibly be positive right now?'

In the darkness, Emma's mother shifted her weight, rustling the sheets. 'Maybe you could make sure the hospice room reminds Nathan of all the things he loves. You could put pictures up and play the music he likes.'

'It just seems so…' Emma didn't want to use the word lame. Her mum was doing her best to be helpful and come up with ideas. 'So inadequate. He was so much more than he is now. I wish we could take him out on one last skydive. It might finish him off, but seeing as the dream is nonsense, I'm sure he'd prefer something like that.'

'Why don't you then?'

'What?'

'Take him on one last flight. If you decide to, I'll help. That boy has given more to me and you than some of our nearest and dearest. The least he deserves is that we try and give some of that back. He did it for me. I'm sure we could do it for him.'

Her mother was right. He'd given them their happy moments. He'd sought to arrange for as many people as possible their everlasting act. The very least Emma could try and do in return was give him something he would enjoy.

A happy ending was nowhere in sight, but Emma was going to do whatever she could to make Nathan's exit one with his own signature style.

Chapter Fifty-Three

Day Ninety-Nine

Staying positive was always more of a challenge when faced with nay-sayers left, right, and centre. Emma hadn't had to ask Nathan's colleagues twice; they were all too happy to help. This wasn't even going to be undercover. It wasn't for a skydive, as Emma had semi-hoped it might be, but even she could see that a man who was practically unconscious most of the time was not a suitable candidate to hurtle through the air. Instead it had been agreed that Nathan would be allowed one last flight. That even if he couldn't jump out the door of the plane, he could be allowed to travel on the ambulance stretcher and at least feel the rush of the wind against his face one final time.

It was the doctors she was struggling to get the sign-off from, and she was losing her patience with them. 'What possible harm is it going to do when he is going to die anyway?' Emma didn't care how loud her voice got. She was pretty certain anyone hearing the conversation would go ahead and back her.

'It's not a case of whether it's the right or wrong thing to do. It's whether we can provide the staff to go with you. I'm not sure we'll get authorised for something like this when it's not standard practice.'

'I'll go,' one of the more junior doctors volunteered. 'I can do it in my own time if it's to do with funding.'

'I'll go, too.' It was the male student – the one who hadn't remembered Nathan's name when he'd first been diagnosed. 'I'll go with Nathan.'

Hallelujah, Emma said in her head. Maybe there was hope if there were still people willing to carry out acts of kindness just when they were needed.

After those first kind gestures, others followed in quick succession. More people volunteered their efforts to assist. Transport was booked and the drivers were more than happy to make an unscheduled stop on the way to the hospice, the doctors volunteering to stay on to finish their work later that day.

When they arrived at the skydiving facility, every member of staff lined up on either side of the door through the building all the way to the plane. It was like a guard of honour, and Emma had to stop a while to compose herself. Although maybe now the time had come to allow herself to cry in front of Nathan. She was as sure as she could be that he wouldn't mind.

Tim and Leanne were the first to greet them, and it was evident in their expressions how shocking the change in Nathan was. Each of his friends greeted him – the ones Emma knew from her mother's skydive and others she'd not met before. They all spoke to Nathan as he passed by on his bed, and it kind of reminded Emma of a funeral in reverse. Nathan was getting to hear words telling him he was the greatest of friends, the funniest person, the bravest of souls, all of which might otherwise have been said only once he was gone. With any luck these sweet footnotes of his life were going in.

The hospital volunteers were pushing the trolley, and after each friend had said their piece, they joined in helping deliver the stretcher towards the waiting plane. The image was so reminiscent of pall-bearers reverently carrying a coffin that Emma had to stop and place a hand over her own mouth to prevent herself from wailing.

It was such a contrast, seeing him here. Catching a glimpse of Nathan on the stretcher was like peering at a different life completely. It seemed nigh on impossible that this was the man who only weeks before had taken her mum skydiving and organised Rudi's indoor jump. The shock in seeing the difference was etched on the faces of all the people there. And Emma was unravelling, no longer sure if she was strong enough to do this.

It was Leanne who came to her rescue. 'My darling girl, thank you so much for bringing him home to say goodbye. You have no idea how much this means to him and us.' Leanne held up a tissue and wiped Emma's tears away like they were lifelong friends. Hopefully they would be. 'Now go and be with him.'

Emma took a breath. Right now wasn't the time for it all to get too much. She needed to be with him. Maybe Leanne was right; maybe for Nathan this was home, at least spiritually if nothing else. His place was always going to be in the sky, because that's where his heart belonged.

Loading the stretcher onto the plane took some manoeuvring, but there were enough people about to make light work of it. The trolley in place, it left room for very few people. There needed to be a medical personnel, according to bureaucracy, and Tim for safety reasons. After that, there was only room for Emma. She wasn't about to let her emotions stop her from taking that spot.

In the plane's cabin, they'd placed Nathan so that he'd have the best view, not that his eyes were open. Tim and the doctor who'd volunteered their time to be there sat further back, allowing Emma and Nathan some time and some space.

As the plane started moving along the runway, Emma decided to talk to Nathan like no one else was there. It was as intimate a moment as she was likely to get with him again.

'I don't know if you realise this, but you've been a little bit of magic in my life,' she whispered. How hard it was to find the things she wanted to say. 'Scrap that, not a little bit, a great big bit of magic in my life. I think you've been that piece of magic for a lot of people. You have a way of making people feel alive. You've made me feel alive.'

The plane was starting its ascent now, tilting off the ground and beginning its diagonal push towards the hazy white clouds – a knitted jumper letting patches of blue show through.

'What I'm trying to say is even though it may feel like it, don't ever think that you've left this life too early. You've had more impact in your twenty-seven years than most people will have in their entire lifetimes. And I'll make sure to do whatever I can to make sure that continues.'

Nathan stroked her fingers. It was more of a response than she'd had for several days, and she knew she would treasure it forever. Half of her willed there to be more, but it was obvious that he was using all his energy to breathe.

'I just want you to know how glad I am that you came into my life. I'm not sure what road lies ahead for me, but I promise you I will do my best to fight. I will do my best to get another twenty-seven years – at least – and embrace them with the gusto you've taught me to have.'

They were up in the clouds now, the plane levelling off as Tim allowed the side door to open. Below, the great expanse of the Salisbury Plain provided views of flat green and yellow fields for miles. If only Nathan were able to appreciate it as much as Emma. She took it all in for a moment… The sound of the gushing wind, the blueness of the skies, the stillness of the earth from this height.

Nathan's eyes were flickering as the wind beat against him. What a sensation it was. Hopefully he would know that, in the same way he'd done everything to ensure her happiness, she was doing the same for him in the only way she knew how: by bringing him here.

It was quite the experience to be so high up with the air pushing its way into every quarter of the hold. She'd never been so exposed. 'You never know. I might end up doing a skydive to raise that money. I think perhaps I could be brave enough for it after all.'

The patchy green fields below them with dots for buildings didn't seem so frightening once she was up here. In fact, the temptation to take up a thrill-seeking hobby was quite understandable from this viewpoint.

The wind was tousling Nathan's hair, but the occasional eye flicker soon faded to nothing. And she wasn't sure if it was from being open to the elements, but Nathan's hand was growing cooler to the touch.

'I love you,' she said, realising before anyone else that this was her last chance to say it.

Nathan offered the slightest squeeze of her hand. She was sure it was real and not imagined.

But then she knew that was it. That the tiny gesture had been the last ounce of energy he had to give.

For a while, Emma remained there in that moment. There was still warmth in his hand, even though she knew he was gone. She wasn't ready to let go, but if the soul was a real thing she needed the door to remain open for a touch longer. If this was the last jump, Nathan's soul needed time to set sail.

There was a beauty in the sky at that moment. It was a bright blue with fluffy white clouds like the type a child would draw. It sang of the start of springtime, of new beginnings, of hope. It was a time for change.

Emma wasn't ready, but then she never would be. Nobody was able to choose this moment and find they would ever be okay with it. But as things went, it seemed an okay way for it to happen.

It wasn't a hospital room. It wasn't where he'd dreamed, for his whole life, about this happening. But it was better than that. It was the place he would call home. His soul would rest easy here. He was finally free.

Nathan

Isn't it the saddest thing that some words will never reach a page? That I can't let you know what's happened to me?

My name is Nathan Foxdale. I will die aged twenty-seven. I have known it all my life. But I never expected you, Emma. I never knew love would exist in my life. How I wish I could talk with you now.

It's really hard to have known when I would die with utmost certainty, only for the dream to not be what I thought.

Interpretation can be a funny thing.

Hospital room… I am ill.

Struggling to breathe… I am dying.

A baby crying… I am a father?

I have lived with these keystones for so long they have become my perceptions of them. And yet here I am again. Although this is not the dream but the reality.

Hospital room… I am being born.

Struggling to breathe… My mother is dying.

A baby crying… My mother is dead. I'm crying for my mother.

Because the dream has never been the end. The dream has always been the beginning. I had twenty-seven years to live. I've lived every hour well. Make sure you do the same.

I'll be waiting for you.

Epilogue

GoFundMe on behalf of Everlasting Acts

I, Emma Green, made a promise to Nathan Foxdale, the founder of the Everlasting Acts charity. I vowed that if I lived past the age of twenty-seven, I would be brave.

In the short time we knew each other, Nathan taught me everything I know about living life to the fullest. On 26 March 2023, I plan to do my first tandem jump. I wish with all my heart that he could be the instructor I will be strapped to as I fall through the air, but I'm pretty sure I'll find him on my way down. I think our daughter believes I will.

Any donations will be going towards the charity he helped set up. His very own Everlasting Act.

Nathan's Diary

Emma

Touchdown. Is that the technical term for it? The moment your feet hit the ground and you become one with the earth again.

I thought it would be soaring through the air that would make me think of you. All of the times you jumped from a plane, and here I am knowing I will only do it once. For all the parts it is made up of, landing was the bit I enjoyed most… Coming home.

I haven't read this diary of yours. Some things are meant to be private, but I hope that writing in it becomes like a wired connection to wherever you are. There are so many things I would like to tell you. Everything from the glorious to the mundane.

But first, the jump!

Do you hear that? I jumped out of a plane!

If I had ever considered chickening out, I couldn't have knowing the amount I was raising – six figures for Everlasting Acts! Our charity is so much more than we ever imagined it would be, with a committee and offices and so many people we've been able to help. Leanne and Tim are in charge of it now. They do it in your name and with your level of gusto, you'd be pleased to hear. It's been an amazing thing to witness.

Mum and I have moved. She's been stable for the last few years and we decided it was time I got to have a house, but we're too used to each other's company. She insisted on having a granny annex to remain in keeping with her granny status.

You would not believe how lucky we got. Juliet is the sweetest child we could have hoped for. She has soft brown curls and the greenest eyes, just like her father. She is eighteen months old and tottering about causing chaos. She has absolutely no fear and she hums when she's happy. This especially makes me smile at breakfast time when I'm not quite awake… Her contented delight when munching on honey on toast is enough to brighten the darkest day. Some days I so wish you could meet her, but then when I see her, I see you. She brings you back a hundred times over.

And there are other things I have back in my life, be it in different ways. I have a new tattooed nipple! It's kind of awesome. It looks 3D but never gives me any bother when it's cold.

Rudi is all set to do his skydive in six months. His sponsorship rockets every day and he is so proud to be able to do it.

You see… so many things to tell you.

So much to say.

But mostly I want to say thank you. The dream that filled your thoughts was the one that made us appreciate every hour while we had them. It has gone on to fulfil so many other people's dreams.

I wish for a day when I can dream of you on repeat.

Until then…

I will listen to the wind when it blows and watch as the earth moves.

I will join in with Juliet when she belly-laughs. I might even start humming at breakfast time.

I will cook the food that we love and eat out in the sunshine. Even in the winter sun.

I will study tiny creatures under rocks and ensure our daughter doesn't eat too many of them.

I will love.

I will laugh.

And above all, I will live. Every day. An hour at a time.

A Letter from Catherine

Dear Reader,

It is such a privilege to know that the words I've written have been read. I want to say a huge thank you for choosing *99 Days With You*. It has come from a special place in my heart and I hope it will find a special place in yours. If you did enjoy it and want to keep up to date with all my latest releases, please sign up at the following link. Your email address will never be shared and you can unsubscribe at any time.

www.bookouture.com/catherine-miller

I hope you loved *99 Days With You*, and if you did I would be very grateful if you could write a review. Every one of them is appreciated. I'd love to hear what you think and it makes such a difference in helping new readers to discover my books for the first time.

I love hearing from my readers – you can get in touch on my Facebook page or through Twitter.

Lastly, please take the sentiment of this story and go and do something with that hour… Book the tattoo. Feed the ducks. Do the thing that makes you happy.

Go live your life with no regrets, and say I sent you.

Love, Happiness and Thanks,

Catherine x

🐦 katylittlelady

🟦 katylittlelady.author

Acknowledgements

This is the first book I've written that I can state has taken several years rather than several months. The story of Nathan and Emma may have never evolved beyond an idea if it hadn't been for the encouragement of my agent, Hattie Grunewald. This is the story she took me on with, and which I promised to write for her, but it wouldn't be as complete as it is without her input.

I owe a massive thanks to Christina Demosthenous and the Bookouture family for falling in love with the story as well and bringing it to the next level, ready for readers to enjoy. A special thanks also goes to Kim Nash for being a stalwart supporter.

For the research elements of this story I have to give particular thanks to Alison Keen, Head of Cancer Nursing at University Hospital Southampton NHS Foundation Trust. I also need to thank friends who shared their treatment experiences: Tracie Gledhill (The Girl With The Boobs blog) and Di Dilly. Without their input, this story wouldn't be as human as it is. Any adjustments made to suit the storyline are down to me as the author. I'd also like to thank YouTube for the many skydiving clips I've watched. I have to confess I am like Emma and have been keeping my feet very firmly on the ground!

I'm incredibly blessed to have such amazing family surrounding me, and this section wouldn't be complete without giving thanks to them. Firstly my gorgeous daughters, Eden and Amber. You both make me incredibly proud and are my reasons to write. A huge thanks to my mum and nan for moving 150 miles to come and live on the same street as me to make my life easier. And because life and stories do move on, I've had the privilege of welcoming Ben into our lives and we all smile more because of it. Thank you to all the Thomson clan for embracing us too. I wish for everyone to be as lucky in life and to get this kind of happy ending.

A big thank you to all my friends who are good enough to know that my head is in the clouds more than fifty per cent of the time and that without their friendship skills I wouldn't be anywhere near as rounded.

Lastly, a massive thank you to all the readers and book bloggers who have supported me during my career. I can only count it as such because of your ongoing support. Thank you. Thank you. Thank you.

Made in the USA
Columbia, SC
30 June 2020